To
Love
Twice

Heather McCoubrey

TO LOVE TWICE

Copyright © 2013 by Heather McCoubrey

Heather McCoubrey
http://heathermccoubrey.com

Cover Photo by bigtim, iStock Photo

Cover Art by Dragonfly Publishing, LLC

Author Photo by Amy McCoubrey

Dedication

Acknowledgements

This book would not be in your hands without the extraordinary assistance of my friends and family.

I would first like to thank my husband, David, and our children for their love, encouragement and patience while I wrote my heart out and followed a dream.

A huge thank you to my beta readers and proofreaders: Darlene, Mel, Carla, Kathy, Vicki, Niki, Heidi, Donna and Colleen. Thank you for your support, ideas, honest critiques and your time. I hope you're all up for round two!

And finally, Sam, thank you for your encouragement, persistence and for helping me remember how much I love writing.

Chapter One

Throwing her hands in the air, Kate walked into the closet and pulled out a suitcase. "I'm done, Brad. I'm just done." Putting it on the bed, she unzipped it and started filling it with the clothes she'd need over the next week. "I can't do this anymore."

"Does this mean you're leaving?" Brad stood in the doorway, blocking her way out.

"Yes, I'm leaving," Kate said, her eyes pleading for understanding. "I can't do this, Brad. It's so obvious I can't be what you need and you make that abundantly clear at every opportunity." Tears streaming down her face, she ran into the bathroom for her toiletries. Her heart was breaking into shattered pieces as she packed her things. All she wanted was for Brad to take her into his arms and tell her things would go back to the way they were before she got pregnant with Mary.

"Well, what are you going to do about Mary?"

"I'm bringing her with me. It's not like you have time to care for her, let alone the fortitude," Kate told him. It made her cry harder to say these words. They'd created Mary out of love, it just didn't make sense that Brad didn't love her anymore.

"What is that supposed to mean?" Brad snapped.

"Brad, you tell me to get a babysitter if I need to use the

toilet or take a shower! You're really going to take care of her now?"

Brad snickered at the idea. "No, I'd hire a nanny," he said matter-of-factly.

"That's exactly my point, Brad." She shook her head sadly. "No, she's coming with me. You won't even notice we're gone." Finished with her own packing, she zipped the bag and put it in the foyer. Picking Mary up, she climbed the stairs to Mary's room to pack.

"What will you do for money?" Brad asked harshly.

"We'll get by. I know how to work. Don't worry, I don't expect anything from you." She finished with Mary's clothes, selected a few of her favorite toys, and then went to the kitchen for Mary's food. Once done with that, she started loading the car. She put Mary in her car seat and went back into the house for her purse, cell phone and keys.

Kate looked at Brad, praying and begging in her heart for him to change his mind, to realize what he was allowing to happen. When he stayed quiet and refused to look at her, she took one last look around her beloved home. Stepping up to Brad, she raised her eyes to his face – memorizing all she loved. Before he could move or know what she was about, she rose up on her toes and placed a bittersweet kiss on his cheek.

"I guess this is goodbye," she choked out, heart breaking as she tried to look into his eyes.

Brad quickly moved to the other side of the foyer. "I won't beg you to stay, Kate. If you do this, if you walk out that door, there's no coming back," Brad said.

His words were razor cuts on her heart. All hope gone, she nodded and whispered goodbye. Opening the door, she quickly walked out of the house and away from her husband of ten years.

Unable to drive for the tears in her eyes, Kate pulled over to the side of the road and called her sister. If there was anyone who could help her sort out the mess her life had become, it was her. "Georgina, I left Brad," Kate cried when her sister answered the phone. Laying her forehead on the steering wheel, she allowed the tears to flow freely down her cheeks.

"You did what? Where are you now?" Georgina asked.

"I don't know, just outside the neighborhood, I think. I can't believe he let us go. Georgie, he didn't even fight me about taking Mary! What kind of man lets his wife and daughter walk out and leave? Didn't he ever love me? Love Mary?" Tears continued to roll down Kate's face as this thought settled on her heart.

"Give him some time to calm down. Maybe he just thinks you're blowing smoke and when you don't come home later, he'll come looking for you both."

"I don't think that'll happen, Georgie," Kate said tonelessly. She repeated Brad's parting words to Georgie. "Do you think that sounds like a man who is coming for his wife and child when he finally calms down?"

"No. But anything could happen, Kate. Come here for the weekend. Let's see what happens."

"Oh Georgie, I can't do that. You've got Tim's family flying in on Sunday. I know you need to get ready for that. I'll go to Mom's."

"What? Are you crazy? Mom'll spend the whole weekend gloating and telling you she was right all along. You don't need that now, especially since you don't know what's going to happen with Brad."

"I appreciate the offer Georgie, but I don't want to intrude. Mary is bound to be fussy tonight since we're away from home," Kate hedged.

"Kate! Mary is the sweetest baby and she'll be fine. Please come, Kate. This is the best place for you right now."

"Alright, Georgie," Kate sighed, giving in to her sister's pleas. "But just for the night. I'll figure out what we should to do tomorrow. See you in ten." Hanging up the phone, Kate wiped the tears off her face and put the car in gear.

Chapter Two

"I think it's a mistake, Kate."

Kate sighed and shook her head. "It's been a month, Georgie. He doesn't want us. I have to move on and I have to be strong. Mary is depending on me." Looking through her clothing choices, Kate realized she had nothing to wear to an interview.

"You're the strongest person I know. I just don't want you to rush into a decision that you'll regret later. We have plenty of space here and there's no reason for you to rush into a job, an apartment, and all that until you know for sure." Georgie stood up and took the clothes from Kate's hand. Gently turning Kate toward her, she looked into Kate's eyes. All she saw was misery. "You're my sister, Kate. I love you and I won't let you go out there before you're sure and ready. You don't owe us anything, we're family. If it makes you feel better, keep a running tab and we'll discuss repayment at a much later date. Right now you need us, Mary needs us."

Tears streaming down her face, Kate reached out and hugged her sister. "I love you so much and I have no idea what I did to deserve you as a sister, but I'll be forever grateful that you are."

"Me too. I'm so sorry he hurt you."

Kate closed her eyes and counted slowly to ten. When she opened her eyes, she had herself under control. "I still want to go on this interview. I need the practice at interviewing, even if I don't get the job. But I need to feel independent and I need to at least know that I can support Mary and me. Can I borrow something to wear?"

"Of course. Come on, let's go raid my closet."

"Ms. Walker! I'm Donovan Campbell. It's such a pleasure to meet you," Mr. Campbell said as he clasped both of her hands with his. "Please follow me," Mr. Campbell gestured down the hall.

As they walked down the corridor, Kate took in the ambiance. The walls were a pale gray, with modern art hanging at two-foot intervals. The carpet was a dark gray berber, with white specks interspersed throughout. The doors were all painted dark gray, the trims painted white. The contrast was amazingly simple, elegant and modern.

Mr. Campbell led her into a conference room, and pulled out a chair for her to sit in. Surprised, Kate stood a moment too long before taking her seat. When was the last time a man held her chair for her?

Mr. Campbell took the seat on the opposite side of the table. "We're just waiting on Ms. McNamara, and then we'll get started. Can I get you some water?"

"No thank you, I'm fine." Kate opened her purse and withdrew her resume. "I have two copies of my resume. Would you like to review it before we start?"

"I actually have a copy here in your file. Keep those though, I'm not sure if Erin has a copy."

Just then, Erin walked in. Kate stood up and shook hands. "Hello Ms. Walker. So glad you could make it in today! How was the traffic?"

"Nice to meet you, Ms. McNamara. Traffic was fine, it was actually moving along nicely. I don't suppose it'll continue that way though."

"Please, call me Erin. No, I doubt it will. Traffic and taxes – two things you can always count on around here!"

Clearing his throat, Mr. Campbell motioned Erin and Kate to sit down. "Thank you again for joining us today, Ms. Walker. The position we're interviewing you for is Executive Assistant. You'll be responsible for Erin completely and will also assist my EA with special projects." Mr. Campbell continued the job description, surprising Kate with the amount of work that would be expected. She had been hoping for a part-time position that paid well, but this sounded much more like a full-time position.

"Excuse me, I'm sorry for interrupting, Mr. Campbell, but I thought this was a part-time position?"

A puzzled look crossed his face. "No, that position has already been filled. Your resume was too advanced for the part-time position. You are more suited to this position. Is that a problem?"

"Well, I'm not sure. I have a small child and I haven't fully investigated child care options."

"Oh, that's easy," Erin interrupted. "We offer a childcare facility here in the building. I have two daughters and they stay here all day with me."

"Is the waiting list long?"

"No, in fact there's always an opening for employees," Erin reassured her.

"Oh, well, I guess that's one item off my worry list. Is it possible to get a tour of the facility?"

"After our interview, I'll take you down there myself. This position will also require some travel." Erin said, taking over the conversation from Mr. Campbell. "I have employees in London. I typically make one trip per quarter and I like to have my EA accompany me. The trip should last a week, Sunday to Saturday. However, the past two trips I've made have been ten-day trips. It all depends on what's going on and what needs to be accomplished," Erin paused and sipped her coffee. "This position is a salaried position, with the potential for an end of year bonus. You are entitled to a two week vacation each year until five years, then it moves to three weeks until ten years and then to four weeks. We have several holidays each year. Our benefits package is one of the best and I can go over that with you later as well. Do you have any questions so far?"

"Is the traveling mandatory?"

"Yes. It's important for you to meet the London employees and to learn and understand all aspects of this part of the company. For you to excel in this position, you'll need to know everything to do with my job."

"And I'm sorry once again, but what is it that you do? I only researched the part-time position since it was what I applied for," Kate said sheepishly.

Erin laughed. "My apologies, Kate. We should have been

more clear when we called to set up the interview. I am the Vice President of Customer Relations. Our products have just launched in the U.K. and that is why I now have a small group of employees there."

"That sounds very exciting! When will you be deciding on the position?"

Erin glanced at Mr. Campbell. "We'd like to decide today. You're our last interview. Let me give you a tour of the daycare facility, give you the information on the benefits and let you get a feel for our company."

"That sounds good. When will you need an answer, assuming you offer me the position?"

"As soon as possible. We need this position filled yesterday," laughing Erin corrected herself. "*I* need this position filled yesterday!"

After touring the day care facility and reviewing the benefits package, Kate was in love with the position. The only thing that worried her was the traveling. If it weren't for that, she'd take the job in a heartbeat. The salary couldn't be beat. She'd have enough to get a small apartment close to the office. She'd already scoped out apartment complexes and most of them allowed for one vehicle, without an extra monthly fee for parking.

Turning into her sister's driveway, Kate felt upbeat and hopeful.

Georgie met Kate at the door with her finger to her lips, and a copy of *People* in her other hand. Smiling, Kate quietly closed the door and set down her purse on the counter.

"*People*? I thought you'd stopped reading those gossip mags?"

"Never! I'm addicted, you know that. Besides, someone has to keep up with current events around here. I wouldn't have anything to talk about at Margarita Nights with the girls!" Georgie laughed and set the magazine on the counter. "So? How'd the interview go?" Georgie asked excitedly.

"Wonderful, but this is the full-time position. They've already filled the part-time position. I was their last interview and they're deciding on candidates today. It sounds so fabulous but it will be lots of work. Oh! And can you believe that they have an on-site daycare facility? I toured it and it looks wonderful. The salary is amazing and the benefits can't be beat. It's perfect except for one thing," Kate said, sighing.

"What?"

"There's a requirement for traveling every quarter for five

to ten days to London. Erin, that's the woman I'd be working for, just hired a group over there. Five to ten days, Georgie, what will I do with Mary?"

"Oh, that's no problem, Kate. We'll watch her," Georgie said matter-of-factly.

"What? Just like that, you're going to offer up your services? Georgie, you can't do that. You haven't even discussed it with Tim!" Kate said incredulously.

Laughing quietly, Georgie hugged her sister. "It's not really a hardship to watch her. And besides, if I know you – you'll find a way to hire a nanny and she'll end up traveling with you, so it'll be a moot point anyway. But until then, we'd be happy to help."

"Well, that nanny idea had crossed my mind," Kate laughed. "I wasn't brave enough to ask about it though."

"It'll all work out, Kate. The job sounds fantastic. You should definitely accept the position, if they offer it to you." She hugged Kate again. "This'll be great for you and Mary!"

Just then, Kate's cell phone rang. Glancing at the caller ID, Kate's eyes popped wide. "It's them," she squeaked.

"Answer it, hurry!"

"Hello, this is Kate." She answered in what she hoped was her best professional tone. Nerves were fighting a war inside her and she had no idea what she was supposed to say or do.

"Hi Kate, this is Erin. I'm calling to offer you the position. Both of us thought your resume was on target. We liked you and thought we all clicked nicely."

"Seriously? You're offering me the job?" Kate looked up to the ceiling and squeezed her eyes closed tight. She couldn't believe it.

"Yes," Erin laughed. "I want you, Kate."

"I accept. Thank you so much! When do I start?"

"How about Monday? That'll give you the rest of the week, plus the weekend to get yourself ready."

"That's perfect. Thank you again."

"Be here at eight. I'll meet you in the lobby and get you set up at the day care center, and then we'll start our day."

"I'll be there. Have a great weekend!"

Hanging up the phone, Kate threw her hands in the air and did a little booty dance. Georgie laughed and joined her. "Time to celebrate, sis! Wine and Chinese takeout tonight. I'll call Tim and have him pick it up on the way home."

Chapter Three

With a relieved sigh, Kate unlocked the door to her new apartment. Mary was babbling in the stroller, content for now with her teething ring. Opening the door, Kate pushed the stroller inside. "Welcome to our new home, Mary!" Receiving more babbling in response, Kate laughed and spun in a circle. They were home! The cozy two-bedroom apartment was perfect for them.

Strolling through the apartment, Kate felt her excitement brimming. Their very own apartment. Space, privacy and independence. Of the three, the independence mattered the most. She would be forever thankful for all Georgie and Tim had done for her and Mary, but she was so happy to be on her own again. It had been a long time since she'd had to take care of herself, and she wasn't entirely sure she could do it. Determined to succeed, not only for herself but also for Mary, she'd taken the job, signed the lease paperwork on her apartment, and put herself out there.

She'd been with the company for a month now and she loved her job. She and Erin clicked so completely, with Kate often knowing exactly what Erin needed before Erin even knew herself. There was always something to get done, always something new to learn and Kate never found herself bored.

But the best part of all was that she could go over to the daycare anytime she wanted and hold Mary. Having no idea what she'd done to deserve this stroke of good luck, she hugged her little miracle closer to her chest and rested her cheek on Mary's head.

Leaving Brad had been the toughest decision she'd ever made, but it was one she was glad she'd made. Two months had passed since she'd left, and she hadn't heard a word from him. Georgie hinted that Kate should call him, just to ensure he wasn't being a stubborn man. Kate knew better. Brad wasn't just stubborn, he was cold and it was obvious from his silence that he was happy they were gone. Kate wasn't surprised at his feelings for her, after all, he'd been pulling away for a year. What surprised her was his feelings for Mary, or lack thereof. Kate honestly thought that he would have gotten in touch with her at least so he could see Mary. But not one word had come from him, and it made her heart hurt to think that Mary would grow up without her father.

Looking down at her little miracle, Kate shook off the dark thoughts. They were sitting in their new apartment. Kate had a great job, and they were both healthy. Dwelling on the thoughts of Brad wouldn't get her through the rest of her life. This was a new beginning for them, and Kate was going to make the most of it!

Pulling out her phone, she dialed Georgie.

"Miss us yet?" Georgie asked instead of saying hello.

Kate laughed, "Of course! What are you up to?"

"Nothing much, watching *Hollywood Reports*. It's kind of quiet and lonely here. Tim just got home from the gym, he's up taking a shower. How are you settling in over there?"

"Oh, we're sitting on the floor, enjoying each other's company. It hasn't hit either one of us yet that we're alone. I imagine once I get her down to sleep, I'll be roaming and wondering what to do with myself."

"Seriously? You'll start unpacking and probably be up until two in the morning. You never were any good at unpacking slowly."

"Yeah, you're probably right," Kate laughed. "Although if I was smart, I'd do exactly that – unpack slowly. I need to be running on all cylinders now that it's just Mary and me."

"You want me to come over and help?"

"No, no, we're fine. I was actually calling to see how Tim would feel about helping me get the rest of our things from Brad's house. I could rent a little moving truck and we could go over there in the morning."

"I'm sure Tim would be happy to help. Let me go ask him real quick," Georgie said.

Kate switched her phone to speaker and set it down on the floor. She reached over and pulled Mary into her lap. She loved the feeling of Mary in her arms. Loved to snuggle and inhale her sweet baby scent. Her little miracle.

"Are you still there? Tim says no problem. He said he'd actually go get the truck in the morning and swing by to pick you up. I'll be there around the same time to watch Mary for you."

"Great! Tell Tim I said thanks, and I'll buy him breakfast in the morning!"

"You'd better buy it before he does the manual labor. My man eats like a football team after he's done any kind of laborious activity," Georgie laughed.

"Well, it's the least I can do. You both have been life-savers and I have no idea what I'd do without either of you!"

"Will Brad be there tomorrow?"

"I hope not. I'm going to call him after I get off the phone with you."

"Well, do that now and call me back. It's better to go into a fight knowing what to expect."

"True." Kate hung up and took a deep breath. Dialing the number that would connect her with her estranged husband, Kate could feel the nerves pressing in on her. She hadn't spoken to him since she walked out of the house two months ago. Not knowing what to expect, she hoped for the best.

"What do you want?" Brad asked rudely.

Unsure how to respond to his tone, Kate opted to state the obvious. "Hi Brad, it's me."

"Yeah Kate, I know. Caller ID?"

"Of course. How are you?" Kate asked timidly.

Brad laughed harshly. "Did you really call to find out how I'm doing?" Brad paused for a moment and then continued in a cold voice. "Come on, Kate. We both know I'm better now than I've been in ten years."

Fighting against the tears and the pain his words caused, Kate closed her eyes and forced herself to finish the conversation. "Of course you are." Kate went quiet unsure how to proceed in the face of his hostility.

"What do you want, Kate?"

"Um, I was calling to ask if it would be convenient for you if I came by in the morning to move out the rest of our things?"

"There's no point. Nothing of yours is here anymore."

"Excuse me?" Kate asked incredulously.

"I told you when you left, there was no coming back."

Understanding finally broke through and with it came intense anger. "You got rid of everything? My clothes and furniture? What about Mary's things?" Kate asked quietly.

"It's all gone, Kate."

"Everything? Brad! How could you do this? What the hell is wrong with you?" Kate demanded.

"Kate, you left. You should have taken your things with you when you left. End of story."

"Brad, you're going to regret this," she said through clenched teeth.

"Are you threatening me, Kate? Really?"

"No, Brad, I'm not. I'm promising you. You will regret the way you've treated me and Mary. You will regret letting us walk out of your life. You will regret getting rid of our things. You will regret becoming the man you have. Make no mistake, Brad. This is a promise. You have gone too far," Kate said. She ended the call, and looked into Mary's smiling eyes. "Oh angel baby, we're up a creek."

Giving herself a moment to compose herself, she put the phone down. She hadn't really thought too much about divorce, and what that would entail. But after this conversation with Brad, she could see she had no other choice. She dialed Georgie, and didn't give her a chance to say a word.

"I need a divorce attorney," Kate said.

"Wow, the conversation went that well?"

"Oh, it went even better. Tell Tim not to bother tomorrow. There's nothing left for us there."

"What?" Georgie exclaimed. "What do you mean there's nothing left?"

"Exactly that. Brad informed me that he cleaned out the house the day after we left. Everything is gone."

"Are you sure, Kate? I mean, that's crazy. Are you positive he's just not saying that, to get back at you?"

"I'm not sure, Georgie. Honestly though, at this point, would you put it past him?"

"Well, no, I guess not. But shouldn't you check to make sure?"

Kate thought for a moment. "Yes, I'd really like to check. But how am I going to do that?"

"We'll just drive over in the morning and check," Georgie said.

"Alright, we'll plan on that. But in the meantime, I want a divorce attorney. Know any good ones?"

Georgie sighed. "No, not personally."

"Me either. I guess I'll Google it. Brad usually leaves around seven-thirty. I have no idea if that's changed over the past two months. I guess we'll find out tomorrow."

"Do you want me to come over tonight?"

"No, that's okay. I'm fine, really. Mary and I are going to eat some dinner, try out the bathtub and then head to bed. Tomorrow is going to be rough. Thanks for the offer, though."

"Not a problem. Call me if you need anything!"

"I will. Good night." Kate hung up and hugged Mary close to her. "Looks like it's just you and me," Kate whispered against her temple.

Chapter Four

As Kate drove up the driveway to her ex-house, she wondered what she'd do if Brad really had gotten rid of everything. She was making a great salary but it wasn't enough to repurchase all she'd lost. Giving herself a mental shake as she parked the car, Kate glanced in the rearview mirror to make sure Georgie was behind her.

Kate stepped out of the car and retrieved Mary from the backseat as she waited for Georgie to join her. Cuddling Mary to her chest, she glanced at Georgie and nodded toward the house. "Here goes nothing." Pulling out her key, she inserted it into the lock and was pleasantly surprised when it worked. "Well, he didn't change the locks," Kate said.

"Wonders will never cease," Georgie said dryly.

Kate pushed the door open and stepped inside. As she took in the foyer, then the living room and on into the bedroom, she wanted to drop to her knees and cry. He hadn't lied. Everything was gone. All of the furniture she'd spent years collecting was gone. The beautiful foyer half-table that she'd found at a flea market was no longer in it's spot. She'd spent hours sanding and staining that table once she got it back home. She'd even replaced the glass in the center because it had been cracked. She'd had to special order the glass, which had taken weeks to arrive.

The bedroom set that she'd scrimped and saved for was also gone, to be replaced with nothing. The mattresses sat on the floor. The house resembled a dorm room in a frat house. Brad was using a milk crate for a bedside table. What was wrong with him?

She moved up the stairs and into Mary's room. Gasping, she clutched the doorframe. Everything was gone. Mary's toys, blankets, the cute floral prints that hung on the wall. All of Mary's clothes were gone, the crib that had once been Kate's, the dresser, rocking chair and the changing table. All that remained in the room was the pink paint on the walls and the white carpet.

Kate was dumbfounded. How could he just get rid of everything? And where did it all go? Bewildered, Kate continued to roam through the rooms. Brad had replaced the dining table with a card table. The couch had been replaced with a Lazy Boy chair. She walked back into their bedroom, his bedroom. She looked around and the tears started to fall.

Ten years! Ten years of her life she'd given to him. Did it not mean anything to him? How could anyone be so callous? So unfeeling? He had turned into a stranger. How could she have lived with him for so long and not known?

"How did I not know, Georgie?" Kate asked in a broken, shattered voice.

Georgie flinched at her tone, slowly shaking her head. "I don't know, sweetie. No one did, you aren't alone."

"But I lived with him. Slept with him. Made a baby with him. How did I not know that he was this monster, so cold and unfeeling?" Kate paused and closed her eyes. She sank to her knees in the middle of the bedroom. In a whisper, Kate continued. "He saved me, Georgie. He saved me and he stayed with me. He didn't know who I was, but he stayed for five days in a hospital room with a woman he didn't know. I know somewhere in there he must have loved me." Kate glanced around the room, completely baffled. "He loved me, married me, made a baby with me. But first, first he saved me. I didn't know he had this in him. How is it possible he kept this part of himself from me?"

"I don't think he did. At least not completely, Kate. You left him. A part of you had to know."

Kate shook her head slowly. "No Georgie. No, I left him because he wouldn't help me. He became distant and rude. He didn't want anything to do with Mary. He would tell me to get a babysitter if I wanted to take a shower. I thought us leaving would wake him up. Make him see that his selfishness was ruining our lives. I thought he was just scared of becoming a father. I thought the nightmares were just his way of working through the fears. God! He was missing so much of Mary." Kate looked around the bedroom. "But this. No, this is something very different, Georgie. This is...this is...I don't know what this is, but it's not Brad. This isn't *my* Brad."

Georgie walked over and knelt down beside Kate. "I know it doesn't help, but you have a chance to start over here, Kate. You've only yourself to please now. You and Mary, you'll be a team, you'll be there for each other. You need to start looking toward the future and away from the past."

"He sat by my hospital bed for five days. Five days, Georgie! He had no idea who I was. I can't wrap my head around this. How do I get past that? How do I get past all we've been to each other?" Kate rested her head on her sister's shoulder and let out a long sigh. "I know you're right, Georgie. And I'll get there, someday. I need time to grieve. When I walked down the aisle, I never expected it to end like this. Never in my wildest dreams. I just wish I understood. I think if I knew the reason, I'd be able to find a bit of closure. It might make it easier to move on and look to the future. This is so hard. I'm not ready for this next part."

"I don't think anyone ever is. But I'm here for you and so is Tim. You'll get through this, we'll help you. You aren't alone, Kate. It appears Brad is thrilled to be alone. Eventually, he might come to regret this. But you. You can't regret this. It's painful now, but you got the best part. You got Mary."

Kate allowed a small smile to break through, cuddling Mary closer to her chest. "Yes I did. She is my miracle. And I need to focus on her. All of this was just stuff. It can't be replaced, each piece was unique and special in a way. But I can collect new stuff. That's something that Mary and I can do together." Kate sighed. "Come on, let's get out of here. There's nothing here for me anymore."

Kate stood and walked out of the bedroom. Taking a last look around the house, she realized the house felt cold, lonely and empty. Exactly how she imagined Brad to be at this moment. She relocked the door and left the key under the mat. There was no point in keeping it, she would never be back.

"Thanks for coming with me Georgie."

"Are you sure you'll be okay? I can have Tim bring me back

later for my car."

"I'll be fine. I think I'm going to go home and finish unpacking Mary's bedroom. I need to do something constructive with all these pent up emotions."

Georgie nodded. She gave Kate one last squeeze before she slid into her car. "Call me later. I love you, sis."

"Love you too." Kate watched as Georgie drove off. She quickly buckled Mary into her car seat and slid in to the driver's seat. Putting the car in reverse, she glanced over her shoulder and was surprised to see a police car parked behind her. The tapping on her window startled her. Rolling the window down, Kate wondered what was going on.

"License and registration, please?"

"What? Why?" Kate asked, confused.

"Ma'am, I need to see some identification."

Deciding to cooperate, Kate reached inside her purse and removed her license. She opened the glove box and removed her registration as well.

A puzzled frown crossed the cop's face as he inspected her documents. "Ma'am, do you live at this address?"

"Not anymore. My husband and I have separated."

"Ma'am, you set off the security system."

"What security system?"

"The one that is installed at this location. I'm sorry, ma'am. It must be something your husband had installed recently. I'm going to need you to come with me."

"What? Are you serious? This is crazy. My daughter is in the backseat. What am I supposed to do with her?"

Glancing in the backseat, his eyebrows rose and he sighed. "If you will cooperate with me, I'll allow you to drive to the police station on your own and I'll follow you."

"I really have to go to the police station?"

"I'm afraid so, ma'am. The security company cannot get a hold of your husband. Until someone speaks to him and gets the safe code, I have to bring you in."

Could this day get any worse, Kate wondered. "Alright, officer. I'll cooperate."

Pacing a trail in the carpet in Tim's office, Georgie vented. "I'm telling you Tim, that house was cold. Empty. It was eerie. And Kate, oh Kate! She just wandered the house with this, this, devastated look on her face. There were a couple of times when I thought she was going to faint. And when she went into Mary's room. God Tim! You've never seen such a desolate look on anyone's face." Georgie sighed and dropped her head into her hands. Tim walked up behind her and rubbed her shoulders. Georgie put her hand on his and held on. Squeezing his fingers, she turned her head to see him. "What makes people do that?"

"I don't know, babe. I don't know."

"She just wants to know why, you know? I don't think she'll ever know. I can see how much that part is eating at her. She's having such a hard time comparing the Brad who saved her with the Brad he's become." Georgie shuddered at the memory of Kate in pain. It had been Brad who'd called her. Kate had been in a coma, and when she woke, Kate had asked Brad to call her. Five long days Kate had been alone. No family, no friends – no one, except Brad. The man who'd saved her. He would always hold a special place in Georgie's heart, because if not for him, Kate may have died.

"Georgie don't. Don't go back there. There was nothing you have done differently."

"That's where you and I disagree, but I'll let it go for now. She's calling a divorce lawyer tomorrow. She's hoping for a quick divorce. She doesn't think he'll fight her for Mary. And she's not going to ask him for anything. I think she's out of her mind. She should at least make him give her child support."

"You think he'd do that? He didn't help her with Mary before she left, you really think he's going to start now?"

"The old Brad would, Tim. You know that. And without him..." Georgie let the thought drift away.

"Georgie, he's been a piece of crap for a year now. Shit, I'm more Mary's father than he is. He doesn't want them anymore and I'll bet you he does what he has to, to get it over and done with quickly."

"I just think he should DO something. But, she should just at least ask for child support."

Georgie's cell phone rang, and she jumped up to answer it. "Hello?"

"Georgie? I need you to come, now."

"What's going on? Kate, is everything ok?"

"No, I'm at the police station. I'm being held for breaking and entering."

"What?! I'll be right there," Georgie hung up, already heading toward the door. She spun around remembering her purse and keys. Not seeing them on the chair, she cursed. "Shit, shit! My keys, where are my damn keys?"

"Right here," Tim held them in his hand. "What's going on? I'll drive."

"The police. She's at the station. Something about breaking and entering. Oh my God, Tim. What is going on?!"

"We'll find out when we get there."

The usual twenty minute drive into the city only took ten. Tim had barely put the car in park when Georgie opened her door and ran for the front door. Rushing through the lobby of the police station, Georgie scanned the room looking for someone to speak to. As she continued down a hall, she looked into a big room full of cops and desks. Spying her sister, she rushed over. "I'm here. What's going on Kate?"

"Oh Georgie, thank God you're here!" Kate walked over and put Mary in Georgie's arms. "They're holding me on suspicion of breaking and entering. They can't get a hold of Brad, and until they do, I have to be here."

"What? That's ridiculous. You're still married. You haven't even filed for divorce yet. How can they do this?"

"Do what?" Tim asked as he joined them.

"Tim, they're holding her for breaking into Brad's house today. Can they do that?"

"I have no idea. But I guess I better get on the phone and find a lawyer." Tim reached in his pocket and pulled out his cell phone. He walked out into the hall to make his call.

"Georgie, I know you will but I still need to ask. Can you watch Mary until this is sorted out? I don't want them to call CPS."

"I'm not even going to dignify that with a response."

"Okay ma'am, your sister is here. We need you to come with us to interview," the police officer said.

"Okay, okay. Um, I don't know what to do," Kate said. "Let me give her a kiss. I'm sorry, Mary. Auntie Georgie is going to watch you. I'll be back as soon as I can. I love you baby." Kate reached out and grabbed her sister, giving her a hard hug. "Thank you so much."

"Don't panic. Tim is calling a lawyer. We'll get this sorted out quickly."

"Okay. Thank you. See you soon."

Georgie watched helplessly as the police officers ushered Kate out of the room and down the hall. She joined Tim in the hall and watched his face trying to read from his expression what kind of luck he was having. He raked his fingers through his hair. Not a good sign. "Right. Thank you anyway. Argh," Tim snarled as he ended the call. "How is it possible that we know every damn person in this city, and none are lawyers?"

"Let me try something," Georgie said. She walked over to the desk and reached into Mary's diaper bag retrieving Kate's cell phone. She didn't know the last name of Kate's boss, but she knew the first name well enough. She read through all the names and finally found Erin under the M's. "McNamara, Erin. Kate's boss. Kate told me that they've really hit it off and become good friends. It's worth a shot."

Georgie hit dial and crossed her fingers.

"Hi Kate, how's it going?"

"Hello, is this Erin?"

"Um, yes. Who am I speaking with?"

"This is Georgie Knight. I'm Kate's sister. I'm sorry to bother you, but we've got a situation. Kate's been arrested and unfortunately we're having some trouble tracking down a lawyer. I know this seems a bit unorthodox, but I'd rather not Google a deadbeat lawyer."

"I'm on it. Is she at the police station now?"

"Yes, they just took her into the interview room."

"I'll be there in fifteen minutes."

Georgie sighed in relief. "Thank you." She ended the call and turned to Tim. "She said she'd be here in fifteen minutes. Here's hoping my idea works," Georgie said as she crossed her fingers. She leaned down and kissed the top of Mary's head.

Chapter Five

Kate couldn't remember ever being so scared in her life. They took her fingerprints, and her picture. She felt like a common criminal. Her hands were shaking and her head felt like a balloon floating above her shoulders.

The officers led her to a tiny cramped room. Inside was a metal table, prominently displayed in the center of the room. One of the officers motioned for Kate to take a seat in one of the four cold, metal chairs surrounding the table. Shakily, she pulled a chair out and sank into it. She glanced up to study the officers who were about to question her while they settled themselves across the table from her.

The first looked like he should have been playing with the NFL. He was tall, bulky and gave the impression he could knock someone over with his pinky finger. His light blue eyes looked strangely out of place in his wide face. His nose was off center, indicating it had been broken more than once. His mouth was wide, his thin lips pulled tight in a grimace. His face was square and she could see his jaw tensing every couple of seconds.

The second one was shorter, and very muscular. She figured he was the type who only did four things: Eat, Sleep, Workout, and Work. His face was lean, his cheekbones prominent. His nose was straight and he had dark chocolate brown eyes. In them, Kate could see the uneasiness he felt.

"Ma'am, I'm Officer Wendle and this is my partner Officer Keegan. We're going to ask you some questions. Do you have any objection to this?" NFL asked her.

"I guess not. Will it help to clear up this misunderstanding?"

"We hope so," Officer Keegan said.

"Alright, then question away," Kate said bravely.

"Ma'am, did you enter the premises of 145 Willow Lane at approximately eight o'clock this morning?"

"Yes. My sister and I went there this morning," Kate answered quickly.

"Did you attempt to disarm the system?"

"No. I didn't know one had been installed."

"Were you aware you were being monitored?"

"No."

"Did you remove anything from the house?" NFL asked her.

"No! There wasn't anything to remove," Kate said angrily. "Wouldn't you or whomever have seen that on the video?"

NFL ignored her question. "Did you go there with the intent of removing items from the house?"

"Yes. Brad and I separated two months ago. I moved into my apartment yesterday and wanted to collect the baby's items, the rest of my clothes and some of the furniture that belonged to me."

"Where have you been living since your separation?"

"At my sister's house." Kate looked off into the corner of the room. She would not cry. She would not lose it in front of these people. She took a deep breath and let it out slowly. She returned her gaze to the officers. Clearing his throat, NFL looked away from her watery gaze and Body Builder's unease was palatable. "Do you have more questions for me?" Kate asked.

Just then there was a knock at the door. NFL got up to open it. Kate almost fainted when Erin walked in. Her hands became clammy and she could feel beads of sweat sliding down her back. What was her boss doing here? Kate rolled her eyes. She could kiss her job goodbye.

Kate didn't even notice the woman who walked in behind her. She was too mortified at seeing her boss. Erin crossed to Kate and sat down quickly next to her. "Are you okay?" Erin whispered to her.

"Y-Yes," Kate squeaked out.

Erin nodded. "Good."

"Gentlemen, my name is Clair Forbes. I need a moment to confer with my client," the woman said. Kate finally looked up and noticed the other person in the room. To say she was tall was an understatement. Kate's eyes kept traveling up and up until they finally reached her face, and then she blinked. The woman was gorgeous. Swimsuit edition gorgeous. Her green eyes danced in her face. Kate could see a tiny sprinkling of freckles across her nose and under her eyes. Her red hair was long and curly. It looked so incredibly thick that Kate didn't think this woman would be able to get a hairband around it.

"Of course," the officers said. They both got up and raced out of the room.

Clair turned to Kate. "What did you tell them?"

"The truth."

"Okay, I need to know exactly what they asked you and what you said in return."

"Why?"

"Because that's my job. Spill it."

Kate looked at Erin, questions in her eyes. Erin nodded toward Clair. "Go ahead, Kate."

"They asked me if I went to Brad's house and they asked me if I removed anything from the house. They asked how I got in and why I didn't turn the alarm off."

"And what did you tell them?"

Kate rehashed what she'd told the officers, right up to the point when Erin and Clair had interrupted. "That's all that was said," Kate finished.

"Okay, I can work with this." Clair pulled out her Blackberry and sent some messages. "Okay, what I need now..."

"I'm sorry," Kate interrupted. "I appreciate you coming here." Kate turned toward Erin. "And I appreciate what you've done for me, Erin. But I'm scared. What's next? This is all just a misunderstanding, at least that's what I keep telling myself."

Clair paused and looked like she was collecting her thoughts. "Okay, here's what I'm hoping will happen. I'm hoping they'll be able to get a hold of Brad soon. I think once they talk to him, this will be cleared up and you'll be able to go home. You don't have a record and since you aren't officially separated from Brad, it's still the marital home. I need to get

a statement from your sister, and that needs to go into the
police file. Once that's done, I'll go work some magic."

"Brad seems so angry, I don't know if he'll let it go when
they do reach him."

"I'm sure he will. After all, the place is empty," Clair said.
"I'll be back soon."

Kate watched Clair walk out of the room and then whirled
in her chair toward her boss. "Erin! I'm so embarrassed. I
wouldn't be at all surprised if you fired me. I'm so sorry that
you're involved. Did my sister call you?"

Erin grinned. "Kate, Kate – calm down! I've worked with
you for a month and you've done nothing to make me think
that you aren't still a good fit for our company." She reached
out and placed her fingers on Kate's arm. "Screw that, a good
fit for me! There is nothing to be embarrassed about."

"But I've been arrested. That can't be good for business."

Erin laughed. "You've been detained and I think that's
different. But whatever. Hell, I've been arrested. I was twenty
and thought I knew everything. I chained myself to a tree on
Harvard's lawn. It was old and diseased, but I didn't think
they should cut it down. There were six of us, all chained to
this diseased, dying tree. What a spectacle. Spent the night
in jail, and got community service. It amuses me now, that
moment in time. Really, Kate, this is nothing. We're behind
you, one hundred percent. Don't worry, everything will be
okay."

"Erin, I don't have enough money to pay her." Kate looked
down at her lap, embarrassed to admit this. "She looks
extremely expensive. And now that Brad has gotten rid of
everything, I just don't see how this is going to work out,
financially. Mary doesn't even have a crib," Kate's eyes welled
up and she willed them away.

Erin reached over and held Kate's hand. "Kate, honestly,
don't worry about anything. Let's get you out of here and get
this mess cleared up and then we'll worry about the money."

"Thank you," Kate whispered.

"By the way," Erin smirked. "She's the best divorce lawyer
in town."

Kate looked up and smiled. "Really?"

"Yes." Erin's smirk changed to a full-blown smile. Her eyes
twinkling she did her best to reassure her friend. "I've got you
covered, Kate."

"Thank you. Really, thank you so much." Kate leaned over
and gave Erin a hug.

There was a light knock at the door, and NFL popped his head in. "You ladies want anything to drink? The coffee is as bad as you see on TV, but the sodas are cold."

Erin spoke before Kate had a chance. "That would be great, two diets if you have them."

"Not a problem." NFL closed the door.

"They've really been quite decent to me. They both look like they'd rather be anywhere but doing this today."

"Yeah, it's nice when you find some really decent cops. Too bad they all aren't like that, right?" Erin laughed.

Laughing, Kate nodded. NFL popped back in the room. "Here you go ladies. You need anything else? Bathroom break?"

"No, I'm okay. Thank you." Kate replied.

NFL nodded and walked out.

"See what I mean? Decent," Kate said. "I hope this isn't keeping you from anything important. Wouldn't that add icing to this delicious cake."

"No, I was just sitting at home catching up on household paperwork. I need an EA for my house stuff too," Erin laughed.

"Well, if I get out of here, you could always hire me. That's how I'll work off Clair's fees. Indentured servitude," Kate cracked a smile.

Erin laughed. "I'm glad to see you still have your sense of humor. If you get out of here and everything gets worked out, I'll think about it. You'd have to bring Mary with you though. My kids would get a kick out of having a real life baby to play with."

"It's a deal," Kate smiled.

Clair stormed into the room. "Okay, they finally got a hold of Brad. He corroborated your story. He said he didn't think you'd actually show up at the house, that's why he didn't tell you about the alarm system. Your sister and everyone is waiting out in the hall for you. Ready to go?"

"Is that it?" Kate asked.

Smiling, Clair answered "Yes."

"Thank you, Clair." Kate looked up, those wretched tears stinging her eyes again. "You'll help me with my divorce?"

"Of course. Erin told me that was the main reason I was here. This was just a speed bump."

Kate stood up, and reached for Clair. The tears wouldn't stay at bay, but Kate didn't care. She was the absolute luckiest woman in the world. Giving Clair a hug, Kate let out a sigh of relief.

Chapter Six

"Kate Walker to see Clair Forbes," Kate told the receptionist. Her palms were sweaty and she felt like she was going to lose the contents of her stomach at any moment.

"Please have a seat. Ms. Forbes will be right out." The receptionist gestured toward the chairs lining the wall opposite the reception desk.

Kate sat down in one of the chairs, concentrating on her breathing. *I will not puke, I will not pass out. I will not puke, I will not pass out.* The litany ran through Kate's head over and over.

Glancing at her watch, she was surprised to see twenty minutes had gone by. She walked over to the receptionist and asked her how much longer the wait would be. "I'm on my lunch break and I don't have much more time," Kate explained.

"I'm sorry, Ms. Walker. I'll call back there again," the receptionist offered.

Kate nodded and went back to her chair. A few minutes later, a woman rushed into the lobby.

"Kate Walker?"

Kate stood up. "Yes, that's me," she said.

"Hello, I'm Sara, Clair's assistant. If you'll follow me, I'll take you back."

"Thank you," Kate said as she followed Sara down the hall.

"I'm sorry for the delay. I don't know who she called to let us know you were here, but it wasn't me! I was just about to call you to see if you were still coming." Sara rolled her eyes. "The girl up front is a temp. Our normal receptionist, Jenny went home. She's pure gold but she was scaring the clients away with her cough. Poor thing was sick as a dog and wouldn't go home until Clair walked out there with the Lysol spray," Sara chuckled.

Kate laughed. "I hope she feels better soon."

"Us too," Sara said dramatically.

She ushered Kate into Clair's office and Kate's jaw dropped. The whole wall was glass and the view of the city was breathtaking. Kate walked to the windows before she could stop herself and took in the the view. She could see for miles. Kate could make out the river snaking it's way through the south end of the city. The skyscrapers were like beautiful sculptures shooting into the sky from the ground. The cars resembled little matchbox cars on the ground and the people were so tiny, Kate could barely make them out. Breathing in, Kate wondered how Clair was able to get anything done during the day.

"Kate! So sorry to keep you waiting," Clair said as she rushed into her office.

Reluctantly, Kate turned from the windows. "How do you get anything done with a view like this?"

Clair laughed, "It's hard some days."

"You must have willpower of steel. I'd never get anything done," Kate laughed as she walked over to shake Clair's hand and then sat down in one of the vacant visitor chairs.

Clair surprised Kate by sitting in the opposite visitor's chair, taking Kate's hand and giving it a slight squeeze. "How are you doing today, Kate?"

"I'm okay if I don't think about it. I've never been arrested...detained...whatever...before, so that was pretty traumatic for me. I've never had to worry about Mary like that. All I could think about was what if I'm thrown in jail?" Kate looked out the window and sighed. "I know my sister would have looked out for her. I let Mary sleep in my bed last night," Kate said sheepishly.

"I probably would have done the same thing. And I hate to say this, but it's going to be a long road and it's going to get tougher before it gets better."

"I know. This whole situation is hard. It's hard for me to reconcile the man I married, with the man he is now."

"Well, we may not get those answers for you, but we will make this situation better for you. Tell me about when things started going wrong," Clair said calmly.

Kate's palms dampened. Wiping them on her slacks, she blew out a breath. "Wow. I'm really doing this, aren't I? That's such a personal question, but I suppose nothing is going to be personal again for a long time."

"No, I'm afraid it won't. I'm hoping we can handle this divorce between the lawyers and just get the judge to sign off on it. But if he fights you on any part, we'll have to go to trial," Clair said softly. "Before we actually start, let me ask you a question. Are you ready for this? Are you ready to take this step? Because once we start, there really is no going back."

Kate took a deep breath and searched her heart. She took the question as seriously as it was asked. She glanced toward the windows again, letting her mind wander. Was she ready for this step? She had to be. Already there was no going back. He'd let her walk out the door. He'd let her take Mary with no fight. He'd gotten rid of everything she owned. There was no coming back from that.

"Yes, I'm ready. I want to take this step. There is no other course for me to take," Kate said quietly but with finality.

Taking another deep breath, Kate started the story. "In order for you to understand when things went wrong, I think you need to know how we met." Kate looked out the window and let her mind go back to that awful day.

"I was a senior in college. MBA program. My father had had a heart attack a couple of days before. He was in ICU and my mother had been staying with him at the hospital. I had finals coming up and a few term papers that I'd needed to work on. I didn't get Mom's voicemail until late. I went by their home, grabbed the things she'd requested and went to the hospital. By the time I had visited, and was leaving, it was very late. My sister was out of town for her best friend's wedding. If she'd been home, she probably would have been the one to handle this and handled it much earlier in the day. She's always been better at handling Mom when there's a crisis. I never had enough patience for Mom. Anyway, it was very late and I normally would have asked a security guard to escort me, but I was tired, and irritated with my mother. God, I was so tired. Between the stress of my father's heart attack, the stress of school and my internship – I was exhausted. All

I wanted was to collapse in bed and sleep for days. I remember arguing with myself, as I rode the elevator, about how much sleep I could allow myself before I got up to cram some more before work." Kate paused and collected herself. "I wasn't paying attention to my surroundings and I'd gotten off on the wrong floor of the parking garage. It wasn't until I got to where my car should have been, that I suddenly realized where I was and why my remote wasn't working.

"As I berated myself for not paying attention, I saw a movement out of the corner of my eye. I flinched, but it wasn't enough. He hit me and I went flying to the ground. He kicked me in the ribs and I could hear them crack. I was so aware of everything that was happening, but I couldn't do anything to stop it. I tried screaming, but no sound came out. I was paralyzed with fear and all I could do was try to protect myself," Kate paused again. Slowly inhaling and exhaling as she ran her fingers over her short, choppy hair. "I had long hair then. He grabbed me by my hair and hauled me to my feet. He punched me in the face and broke my nose. I would have fallen, but he still had a hold of my hair. He threw me up against a car and punched me in the stomach and then hit me in the face again. This time I went down. My ears were buzzing, my vision was going black and all I could do was lay there on the ground. I know I was whimpering because he told me to shut up. He dragged me between the two cars and straddled me. He grabbed a hold of my throat and squeezed. He told me that if I made one sound, even a tiny whimper, he'd strangle me. I nodded my head as much as I was able. He ran both hands down my chest and lifted my shirt. I was wearing sports bras then because they were more comfortable than my regular ones. He sneered when he saw it and pulled that up as well. I was panicking. I didn't want to be raped, no one does, and I didn't know how to get myself out of this situation." Kate reached up and brushed away the tears that were running down her face. "The light was dim in the garage and my eyes were swelling up. I really couldn't make out his face, but I knew I needed to memorize what he looked like. I stared and stared at his face trying to commit each feature to memory. He was squeezing my nipples and I remember how much it hurt and all I wanted to do was scream and scream for help. He grabbed my throat again and started to slide my pants down my legs. He was getting his pants down when Brad showed up." Kate paused, taking several deep breaths to calm herself down.

"Would you like some water?" Clair asked hesitantly.

"Please." Kate took a deep drink of the ice cold water Clair handed to her.

"Take your time, Kate. We have as much time as you need."

Nodding, Kate took another drink of water. "It's just not something that I actively think about everyday. And when I do think about, or talk about it, it all comes rushing back and I'm there again. Broken, helpless and scared. No one likes feeling that way, and I know that. And I try not to feel sorry for myself, there's so many people out there who got it worse." Kate took another sip of water and continued. "I was so scared. I thought Brad was with this guy. I knew I wouldn't survive it. My eyes were swelling shut and my face couldn't register the shock and fear of Brad appearing. I've never seen someone move so fast. Brad took his briefcase and bashed the guy upside the head. He fell into the car next to us and jumped up. Brad threw his briefcase on the ground and dropped into a fighting stance. The guy who attacked me took a swing at Brad. Brad ducked and came up with a punch to the guy's face. I don't know how long the fighting went on, it seemed like forever. I was so scared, I didn't move. I felt like if I moved and my attacker won the fight, it would be worse for me if I wasn't exactly as he left me.

"Brad got a few good punches in, before another man drove up and joined the fight. I found out later that Brad was there with his brother, Michael, visiting their sister who'd just had a baby. Michael called the cops and then jumped out of his car to help Brad. Michael didn't even know I was there until after they'd gotten my attacker under control. Brad left my attacker with his brother and came over to help me cover up. And it was then that I was finally able to scream. I screamed until my voice went hoarse. I was backed up against the wall, my clothes all askew and my arms held out in front of me. My legs were curled up to my chest and I wouldn't let him come near me. He knelt down in front of me with his hands out. I could see his lips moving, but I had no idea what he was saying. All I knew was that he was a man and I wasn't letting him come near me. When the cops showed up, it was even worse. They both were men and I wouldn't let them come near me either. I just kept screaming when they would look at me or try to come near me and then whimper when they backed off. My brain, it was like it had shut off. Other than the screaming and whimpering, I couldn't do anything else. I was sitting there, crouched up against the wall, my clothes hanging off me and all I could do was scream.

"Someone finally had the brains to call in a woman cop and someone from the ER. They came running, a nurse and a trauma doctor. And thankfully they were both women. They scooted past the cops and Brad and knelt down in front of me. I knew they were women, I knew they were speaking to me and asking questions but I couldn't respond. All I could do was look at them. The doctor told the nurse to go get a stretcher. When she got back, the doctor and nurse helped me onto the stretcher and pushed me back to the hospital. The next thing I remember was waking up in a hospital room. The sun was shining and Brad was sleeping in the chair next to my bed. I learned later that I had been in some sort of coma for five days. I'd had a fractured skull and they figured the injury plus the trauma made my brain shut off. It was very strange, because as scared as I was of him that night, when I saw him in the chair next to my bed that day I wasn't scared. I felt protected. And I knew that I would get through this. I'd make it out the other side and I'd be a different person for it, maybe even a better person. Time heals all wounds they say. God, I heard that so many times during my group therapy sessions. It doesn't "heal" them, it just fades them. They're like scars on your soul. And this, this was a major scar. But there he sat and even though I had no idea why he sat there, or even who he was, he gave me something tangible to hold on to. I know that sounds weird," Kate finished.

"No, it doesn't. I completely understand what you're saying," Clair said.

"I must have made a sound because his eyes snapped open. His face looked startled, like he wasn't expecting me to be awake. I tried to smile at him, but my face was still a mess and I imagined it looked pretty gruesome.

"He put his hands up and whispered 'Don't panic, I'm not here to hurt you.'

'I know. I remember you.'

'How do you feel? Do you want me to buzz the nurse?'

'Not yet. What's your name?'

'Brad. I'm Brad.'

'Thank you Brad.' Some tears escaped then and when he saw them he panicked. He pressed the buzzer on the bed remote for the nurse. When she came in and saw me awake, she immediately went back out for the doctor. Brad started to get up, but I asked him to stay. He was the only familiar face

I knew. He asked if he could call anyone for me and I asked him if he'd call my sister, Georgie. Of course, ironies of ironies, my mom and dad were still in the hospital but they had no idea that I was there too. They hadn't really worried too much when I never answered the phone, they knew about my term papers and finals and I was notorious for avoiding all distractions when I need to. Anyway, I gave him Georgie's name and number and when the doctor came in, he slipped out to call her. He came to see me everyday that I was at the hospital. He came to see me everyday when I went home. He would sometimes cook for me, he'd go to therapy with me, he'd go grocery shopping with me. We were inseparable. It was just natural that we get married. So we did. Exactly one year after my attack, we got married." Kate smiled dreamily as she brought back the day of their wedding. "I picked the day. Brad wasn't sure at first. He didn't think it would be smart to have our wedding anniversary on that same day. But I told him that even though that was my absolute worst day, it had also been my absolute best day. It had brought him into my life. And that, well, that was something to celebrate." Tears began to pour down Kate's face. She reached for the tissue that Clair held out to her. "I just wish I knew why. Why did it change?"

"That is an incredible story," Clair said softly. "You both have a lot invested in each other. Are you sure you want to do this?" Clair asked again.

"I don't see any other way," Kate said sadly. "Going back and reliving that. It brings back all the best memories. All of our best times. But he doesn't want that anymore. He's different. He's not that man anymore. I don't know why. It was a little more than a year ago. Right after we found out I was pregnant. Brad's always been a little moody at times. He explained them away as his "moments of panic," when he'd relive my attack. Sometimes it was his moments of panic and other times he was just grumpy. Then he started having nightmares and in those nightmares, he never got there in time to save me. We started going to therapy together since we were now both having nightmares. The therapy helped and we gradually stopped going.

And then the nightmares came back for him. But this time, it wasn't just me being attacked. He was picturing me pregnant and being attacked or sometimes I'd be walking to my car with the baby in my arms. I suggested therapy again, but he didn't want to go. He said they'd go away, that it was so easy to explain. Just old fears resurfacing and mingling with new fears. So I let it go. The closer and closer I got to delivering, the worse the nightmares got. He started sleeping on the couch. And then one day he came home from work and it was like a switch had been thrown. He was rude. He was critical. He would ignore me. He stopped sleeping in our room, preferring either the couch, or later, his office. He stopped coming home for dinner. Most nights, he'd wait until I was already in bed. And then he'd be gone before I was up in the morning. I'd see him briefly on the weekends. He wouldn't talk to me. I begged and pleaded for him to tell me what was wrong, but he just ignored me. I loved him so much and I couldn't find a way in. I couldn't reach him. And then it was time. I went into labor. I called his cell, his work, his friends. No one knew where he was and he wasn't answering his phones. I called my sister. She and I went to the hospital. Her husband tracked Brad down. He was at home, drinking. Tim dragged Brad to the hospital. Brad made it just in time to see Mary born. I remember feeling so thrilled that he made it in time. He'd held my hand, he'd gazed at Mary. Had brushed his fingers over the downy softness of her hair. He'd even held her once they'd cleaned her up. And when they moved me to my private room, he would just hold her and gaze at her. He'd look at me and sometimes there would be tears in his eyes. He'd sit with me on the bed and we'd hold hands and just stare at her. I thought things were back to normal. I thought that maybe all that had happened had just been him freaking out and not being able to talk about it. Until we went home from the hospital. And it all started again. I'd ask him to hold her while I heated her bottle and he wouldn't. I'd ask him to hold her while I went to the bathroom and he wouldn't. I'd ask him to watch her while I took a shower. He'd tell me to get a babysitter. I was exhausted and I knew she could feel the tension. She was fussy a lot and it irritated him that she cried so much. She didn't sleep well unless he was out of the house. I didn't sleep well unless he was gone. It had all flipped. There had once been a time when I couldn't sleep unless he was there. And now, I couldn't sleep unless he was gone. I couldn't even relax unless he was gone. So, I packed our things and left him. And now, here I sit, ready to divorce him. I'm scared to death. But I see no other option."

Clair took Kate's hand in hers. "That's where I come in. I'll be here for you every step of the way, Kate. And I'll do my absolute best to try to keep this out of the courts. Have you thought about any of the details?"

"The only detail I've thought of is whether he'll sign away his rights to Mary. If he's going to continue being the way he is, then I don't see why he should get a say in anything regarding Mary."

"If you do that. If you allow him to sign away his rights to Mary, you'll get no child support."

"I know. And I'm okay with that."

"Okay. What about alimony?"

"No alimony."

"I assume you want sole custody of Mary. Do you want to come up with a visitation schedule?"

"A visitation schedule? Isn't that contradictory to him signing away his rights?"

"Yes, but it's best if we have all the angles ironed out before we serve him with the divorce papers."

"Oh, in case he decides not to sign away his rights, I understand. Well, I hadn't really thought about any visitation schedule. What is normal?"

"Usually, the non-custodial parent will see their child once or twice during the week and then the parents will switch off weekends, holidays and school vacations – which of course doesn't apply yet."

"That sounds fine to me."

"Okay." Clair asked Kate more questions, scribbling notes as they went along. Kate breathed a sigh of relief when Clair said they were done. "I'll have my assistant type up the documents. I'll need you to come back tomorrow to sign them and then we'll have them delivered to Brad."

"Okay. I can swing by on my lunch break tomorrow. Do you mind if I bring Mary with me?"

"Not at all. You won't be here long, just long enough to sign the papers," Clair assured her.

Kate stood up and shook Clair's hand again. "Thank you so much. I'll see you tomorrow."

Chapter Seven

Kate was a nervous wreck. She'd been disorganized and distracted all morning. Twice Erin had to poke her head out of the office and ask Kate if she was going to answer the phones. She'd even misplaced Erin's presentation this morning. They both had been searching Kate's space when Kate had discovered the presentation in the recycling bin. "I'm so sorry, Erin."

"I know and it's fine, Kate. I know today is impossible for you. Why don't you go to lunch early. Get Mary, enjoy some lunch and then go sign the papers. You won't have your head on right until it's done."

"You're sure?"

Erin laughed. "I'm sure. I'll be in the meeting anyway and last I checked the voicemail system was still working."

"Alright. I'll see you later this afternoon. Thank you."

Erin turned to leave. When she got to the door she turned back. "Kate, if you get done with those papers, and you're wrecked, please take some time off and go home. I honestly can live without you for the rest of the day. Sometimes the best place for us is in the comfort of our homes. So if you need to, just go home after. I'll understand."

All Kate could do was nod. She could feel the tears

threatening and her throat felt swollen shut. Erin smiled at
Kate and then walked away. Kate stared after her and again
wondered what she'd done to deserve this job and Erin.
Somewhere along the way they'd become friends.

After tidying her desk and locking her computer, Kate put
on her jacket and grabbed her purse. She called the daycare
to tell them she was on the way and then walked to the
elevators. She would do as Erin had suggested. She'd get
Mary, grab some lunch and then go to Clair's office. She
wasn't incredibly hungry, but she thought a nice bowl of
Cheddar Broccoli soup from Panera's might be enough to get
her through the rest of the afternoon.

"Kate Walker for Clair Forbes," Kate told the receptionist.
"Please have a seat, I'll let Ms. Forbes know you're here."
"Thank you." Kate walked over to the chairs and sat down.
She unfastened Mary from her car seat and took off Mary's
jacket, placing it in the car seat. Mary's legs were getting
stronger and she loved to balance on Kate's lap. Kate would
hold her upright and Mary would bounce and stand on Kate's
legs. Today it seemed that Mary was more interested in her
surroundings than balancing on Kate's legs. There was a
picture behind Kate's head that had captured Mary's
undivided attention. Kate turned to look at it and could
understand why. It was a modern abstract painting with
circles, squares and triangles all colored red, white and black.
Kate was having a hard time keeping Mary's hands away from
the painting and was happy when Clair's assistant Sara
arrived.

"Hello Kate, sorry to keep you waiting."
Kate smiled. "Not a problem. Although I may have to take
this painting home with me. Mary seems to love it."
Sara laughed. "I'll let Clair know. No one would miss that
painting, I'm sure. I mean what's it even saying? Squares,
circles and triangles, that sounds more up Mary's alley than
ours."
"You're right. What's wrong with you guys? Art for babies
in your reception area. What kind of statement are you
making?" Kate and Sara laughed. Sara led Kate into Clair's
office.
"Clair is stuck in a deposition, but asked me to get you to
sign the paperwork. She also wanted me to ask you one last
time. Are you sure you want to do this?"
Kate sighed. She'd kept herself up most of the night

wrestling with this same question. After spilling her guts to Clair yesterday, the memories had been swirling around in her head, unwilling to go back into their box in her mind. She'd reminisced while she drank some wine after putting Mary to bed. She'd gone back and forth and all she could come up with was ending it. There wasn't anything left in her that pointed toward any hope of reconciliation. The Brad she'd fallen in love with was gone and Kate wasn't willing to risk Mary's happiness and well-being waiting to see if the old Brad came back. If not for Mary, Kate's answer may have been different.

"Yes, I'm sure. But before I sign the papers, I just have one question. What if these papers snap Brad out of wherever he's been? What if he wants us back? What happens?"

"This is more of a question for Clair. Let me see if she can be interrupted to come talk to you or at least give me the answer."

"Okay, thank you." Kate chided herself for being weak enough to ask that question. It didn't hurt to know all the angles, but at the same time Kate couldn't see Brad changing. And she was just setting herself up for a bigger fall when he didn't come crawling back.

Sara returned quicker than Kate expected. "She said if that happened and you wanted to stop the divorce, we could do that. She did say, however, in her opinion, you should contact her immediately if that were to happen. She said sometimes it's a trick. Not that Brad would do it, but that she'd seen it once or twice happen to a client. She said the best thing would be counseling before dropping the divorce entirely."

"Thank you, Sara. I just wanted to make sure there was an out if needed. I doubt there will be, but you never know. Where do I sign?"

"I've marked all the spots that need your signature. Here's a pen. Do you mind if I hold Mary while you sign the paperwork? I'm in desperate need of a baby fix," Sara smiled.

"No, not at all. Do you have children?" Kate asked.

"Yes, three of them. One in college and the other two are in high school. It's been so long since I held a baby and I know it'll be even longer before I hold a grandchild. I have all boys. They aren't notorious for marrying early and having babies," Sara laughed. "I live vicariously through other people's babies. Oh! I miss that baby smell. I wish it could be bottled," Sara sighed.

"Yes, I know what you mean," Kate smiled. She watched Sara dance over to the windows to show Mary the view. Kate watched Mary's reaction for a minute and then got to work signing the paperwork. After signing, she flipped back through the pages to make sure she got them all. "I think I'm all set here, Sara. Do you want to double check my work?"

"Yes. Clair will not be happy if we have to call you back in," Sara said. She snuggled Mary closer. "Oh, I don't want to give her back to you. She is such a darling!" Sara handed Mary back to Kate. "Thank you for sharing her." Sara looked through the paperwork and couldn't find any spot Kate missed. "This looks good. I'll leave it on Clair's desk. She'll review it again just to be sure. If it's good to go, it'll be delivered to Brad today."

"Wow. Today? Is that normal?"

"Yes. It's best to get these things out and rolling."

"Makes sense," Kate said as she gathered up her purse. She'd left the car seat out in the reception area. "Thank you for your help. Will I hear from Clair soon?"

Sara walked Kate out to the reception area. "Yes, as soon as Brad's lawyer contacts Clair, she'll let you know. If Brad calls you, just refer him to Clair, especially if he's not being nice."

"Okay. I will." Kate put Mary's jacket on her and then buckled her into her car seat. She picked up the car seat and her purse and shook Sara's hand. "Thanks again. I'm sure I'll talk to you soon," Kate smiled.

"Take care, Kate."

Kate walked to the elevators. She couldn't get a handle on her emotions. She was sad, relieved, angry, and happy all at once. It wasn't until she had Mary in the car and herself buckled in that the tears came. A steady stream of tears rolled down her face. She rested her head on the steering wheel and let them wash through her.

A light knocking on her window jolted her. She looked up and saw a petite woman looking at her curiously. "Are you okay, dear?" The woman asked through the window.

Kate quickly rolled down the window. "Yes, I'm fine. Thanks for asking. It's been one of those days," Kate explained.

"Oh, I know what you mean. Take care," the woman said.

Kate started her car and decided that the last place she wanted to be was back at work. She headed for the comfort of home.

As she drove home, her thoughts continued to be dominated by Brad. She admitted to herself that she missed him. Missed him so much it was a constant ache in the center of her heart. She missed their chats, missed snuggling with him on the couch watching movies, missed lazy weekend mornings.

She tried to figure out where it all went wrong. She probably wouldn't be able to fix it, but if she just knew, she might have a chance at fixing it. All she wanted, truly wanted, was her life back. Her husband, her baby's father. What had gone wrong?

She pulled into the parking garage and hurried to the elevator with Mary. Kate called Georgie to tell her it was done, the papers were on their way to Brad. Georgie offered Kate her sympathies and a shoulder to cry and/or vent on. Kate declined, preferring to be alone with Mary until she went to bed. Then Kate planned to drink a tall glass of wine and soak in the tub before going to bed herself. Because really all she *wanted* was this day to end. All she *wished* for was to wake up from this nightmare.

Chapter Eight

Brad opened his door to a messenger. His heart lurched as he realized what the messenger held out to him. "Sign here, please."

Brad signed on the line, muttering, "Thank you," when he passed the clipboard back to the messenger. Shutting the door, he opened the envelope and pulled out the papers. She had finally done it. Kate had filed for divorce. He sat heavily on his bed and cradled his head in his hands. It was better this way. Better that Kate hated him and Mary didn't know him. Kate could move on, meet someone new and live a long happy life. Whoever Kate chose to enter her life would treat Mary the way she deserved to be treated. As a daughter. All Brad would have given her was heartache and pain.

Slowly, he raised his head. The pain in his heart was intense. He had wanted to wait. Wait until Kate gave up on him. And now that the time had come, he could finally end all his pain. Forever.

He laid back on the bed. God, he missed Kate. Closing his eyes, he relived the past ten years. The night he found her. The long scary days in the hospital waiting for her to wake up. The blissful and bittersweet year after the attack. Their wedding. Their honeymoon. Their home. The minutes, hours, days, weeks and years in between then and now. He'd been lost and alone when Kate had entered his life. She'd filled it so perfectly that a day hadn't gone by his cup didn't spill over from happiness.

And then he'd visited the doctor. It had been a week after they'd found out Kate was pregnant. God, she'd been so beautiful. And they'd celebrated the news with a lovemaking marathon that lasted two days. Blissful. He was so happy. He didn't even care what sex the baby was. So long as it was healthy, it would be perfect. He'd been looking forward to being a father. To prove that it could be done right. To prove that he wasn't anything like his father.

Then he'd received news he'd never wanted to hear. Cancer. Stage four. Terminal. And so, he'd had to be strong. Strong enough for all of them. Kate would have wanted him to fight. He could picture how she'd be, in his face, demanding that he fight. Fight for her, fight for the baby and fight for himself. For their life. Their precious life.

He couldn't though. He never told her the diagnosis. Of course, she hadn't been aware that he'd even gone to see the doctor. The doctor gave him a year, two at the most. He'd given Brad the standard lines about treatment. But they both knew the truth. No matter what they did treatment wise, Brad was still facing a death sentence. And he wasn't going to impose that on his wife and new baby.

He started pushing her away, but she clung to him and their life. He didn't let her off the hook and he kicked it up a notch. She just wasn't getting it. She wasn't letting him push her away.

He allowed himself a minute to imagine what Mary looked like. She was almost six months now. She was probably sitting up, rolling over and maybe even crawling. He bet she looked just like her mother. She'd be a beauty for sure. He stifled a sob at the thought of never seeing her grow up. Watching her graduate. Walking her down the aisle on her wedding day. Of holding his grandchild. Of growing old with Kate.

The pain of those thoughts tore through his soul. He curled in on himself to hold it at bay. It would never ease. This intense pain of loss. And now that Kate had given up on him, he could finally find peace in the end of his life. He knew it was near. The pain in his head was never-ending, no amount of pain pills dulled it. His vision was blurry most of the time and he had no appetite, which showed in the fifteen pounds that had disappeared off his frame in the past couple weeks.

Brad rose from the bed and went to his dresser. Collecting the letters he'd written over the weekend, he put them in his pocket and walked to the kitchen. Michael was supposed to stop by soon and Brad could imagine the earful he was going to receive, especially once Michael found out about the divorce papers. He didn't have the energy for the visit tonight, but Michael would show, come hell or high water. Brad grabbed a beer out of the fridge and walked out onto the back deck. He sat down heavily in the deck chair and took a sip of his beer. From his shirt pocket he pulled out the one thing he'd kept. It was a picture of Kate, Brad and Mary at the hospital, minutes after Mary had been born. Closing his eyes, he kissed the picture, and tears streamed down his cheeks. He missed them so much, time didn't ease the pain. It only increased the pain.

Brad leaned his head back against the chair and gazed into the sky. Twilight was settling in, darkening the sky and washing the clouds in a rainbow of beautiful colors. Brad's eyes were drawn to the first star of the night. Smiling slightly, Brad remembered Kate's penchant for making a wish on that first star every time she saw it. Brad closed his eyes and made his own wish on the star. He wished for Kate to forgive him and for her and Mary to find happiness.

He lifted the bottle to his lips, cursing when it slipped out of his fingers and crashed to the deck floor. He sat up to retrieve the bottle and was blinded by pain exploding in his head. Falling back against the chair, he tightened his hold on the picture. He raised it to his lips again and then allowed the darkness to take over.

"Brad?" Michael called as he prowled through the house, turning on lights. "Brad, where the hell are you?"

Michael opened the screen door and froze. "Brad," he whispered. His eyes raced over his brother and took in the scene. Brad was slouched in the deck chair at an odd angle, eyes closed. The beer bottle shattered on the deck floor. He reached into his pocket and dialed 911 as he moved through the door and put his fingers to Brad's neck.

"911, what's your emergency?"

"I need an ambulance at 145 Willow Lane. There's something wrong with my brother."

An hour later, Michael stared at the doctor, pain slicing through his heart. Words he never expected to hear, flowing from the doctor's mouth.

"I'm sorry, there's nothing more we can do."

"I don't understand," Michael said to the doctor. "I had no idea he was sick."

The doctor nodded. "I know, it was his wish. I diagnosed him with an inoperable brain tumor a little more than a year ago. By the time I saw him, it was already Stage Four. He's been managing the pain with pills."

"Why wouldn't he get some sort of treatment?"

"Because he knew it wouldn't help. I asked and asked. He didn't want anything. He said he was staring at a death sentence, no matter what we did."

"Stubborn ass!" Michael fumed.

"We can make him comfortable with morphine until he passes. I doubt it will be long now." The doctor reached into his coat pocket and removed some envelopes and a picture. "These were with him when they brought him in, I thought you'd want them."

Michael took the envelopes and quickly scanned them. Four envelopes all addressed to a different person. One for Michael, one for their sister, one for Kate and one for Mary. "Shit," Michael whispered to himself. "He's put his affairs in order. He knew."

Michael stuffed the envelopes in his coat pocket and looked down at the floor. Taking a deep breath, he let it out slowly, giving the emotions a chance to pass. "Can I see him?" Michael asked in a ragged voice.

"Yes. He won't be conscious, but it's a good time to say your goodbyes."

The ringing of the phone woke Kate from a fitful sleep. She couldn't quite grasp what she'd been dreaming, though she knew it hadn't been good.

"Hello?"

"Kate? It's Michael."

"Michael?" Kate glanced at the clock and sat up. "It's two in the morning, Michael. What's wrong?"

"Come to the door, Kate. I'm outside. Please let me in."

"I'll be right there, give me a second." Kate pulled on her robe and went to let her brother-in-law in. Soon to be ex-brother-in-law. Kate peeked out the peephole to ensure Michael was alone. She unlocked the door and opened it. "Michael? What's going on?" She led him over to the couch and sat down next to him.

He took hold of her hand. "Kate, it's Brad. He's...he's gone, Kate."

Kate's face paled and she squeezed his hand. "Gone? What do you mean, gone?"

"Kate, he died tonight."

"Died? Michael, are you sure? What are you talking about?" Kate snapped angrily. "What's really going on, Michael?"

"Kate, look at me," Michael said sharply. "Kate, he's gone. I-I saw him." Michael closed his eyes. His voice dropped to a whisper that Kate could barely make out. "I found him, Kate. We had plans tonight. We were planning to go out and get a drink. I planned to grill him about you two and kick his ass a bit for letting you go. I had to work late, so I left him a message, telling him I'd be late.

I got to the house around ten. It was dark, and I didn't think anything of it. I figured he was out on the deck drinking a beer," Michael hung his head, shook it and relayed all that had happened that evening, ending with passing her the envelopes that Brad had left behind for her and Mary.

She barely glanced at the envelopes, dropping them on the couch next to her. Kate flung his hand away and stood up, her eyes darting around the room.

Michael stood with her and placed his hand on her shoulder. "Kate, please sit down. Can I call someone for you?"

Kate eyes stopped darting and settled on Michael's, widening slightly. "Oh my God, you're serious? He's dead?" She asked in a whisper. "NO! Michael, NO! NO! Stop it. Stop this! He can't be dead, Michael. I still love him. I'd know." And just that quick her dream, no nightmare, came back to her. Brad standing in front of her. Clutching a photo of the three of them and telling her goodbye. 'I'm so sorry I had to hurt you, Kate. I love you. I always have and I always will', he'd whispered right before the ringing of the phone had woken her up. Kate reached out, grasping at the air. "NO!" she whispered. "NO!" Dimly she heard Michael calling her name. She couldn't focus. The room was spinning. He was gone? How could he be gone? What had she done? Why? Her mind couldn't grasp it and then it all went black.

"Kate? Honey? Open your eyes," Georgie said as she patted Kate's cheeks.

Keeping her eyes closed, Kate whispered "Brad's gone.

He's never coming back."

Georgie took Kate's hand in her own. "I know, baby. I'm so sorry."

"Why didn't he fight?" Kate shook her head. "I can't focus, Georgie. I can't open my eyes, because it'll be real then. I don't want it to be real, Georgie." Tears started to leak through her eyelids. It didn't take long for them to become giant racking sobs. Kate curled herself into a ball.

Georgie laid down next to her and wrapped her arms around Kate. Rubbing Kate's back, she whispered "Let it out, let it out."

Kate had no idea how long they lay like that. Slowly, reality crept back in. She wondered where Michael was. Had he left after calling her sister? She assumed he called Georgie. "How did you find out?"

"Michael called in a panic."

"How long have I been out?"

"Well, it took me fifteen minutes to get here."

"Is Mary still sleeping?" Kate's heart broke thinking that Mary would never have a chance to know her father.

"Yes," Georgie whispered.

"I don't know what to do. I don't know what to feel. I still can't focus on it. It hurts so much."

"I know it does. You don't have to think of it yet. Just stay put. You don't need to rush into it."

Kate squeezed her eyes tighter. Could she have done anything? Could she have prevented this? Oh, how was she going to make it through this. It was impossible. Impossible to open her eyes and face reality. To face her life without Brad. To know that he was never coming back. There was no hope that they'd find each other again. It was well and truly over.

It rained the day of the funeral. Kate found this a fitting predicament. She'd been crying all morning. Kate's mother had come to watch Mary while Kate attended the funeral. She didn't want Mary around so much sadness. The service had been beautiful. Michael had planned most of it. He'd asked Kate to help him, but she'd turned him down. She could barely take care of herself and Mary for the grief, there was no way she would have been able to help with the arrangements. Michael had thankfully understood.

Erin had told her to take as much time as she needed. Kate would have loved to bury herself in work, but she could barely get herself out of bed. All of her energy went to making sure Mary was taken care of everyday. It had only been a week since Brad died, but she'd lost enough weight that her clothes hung on her frame. Dark circles were a permanent addition to her eyes.

Kate walked slowly down the hall to her apartment. She walked in and closed the door behind her, closing her eyes and leaning up against the door. More tears fell unchecked down her face. They were never-ending.

"Kate, dear?"

"Hi Mom," Kate whispered.

"What can I do, Katie?"

"I don't know, Mom. I don't know how to get past this. Time, I suppose. Isn't that what they always say?"

"Oh, Katie – I hate to see you in so much pain. You've had more than your fair share already."

"My lot in life, I guess. Do you mind staying for a little longer? I want to take a bath. I need to pull myself together."

"Of course, dear. I'll stay as long as you need me. I found two envelopes stuck in the couch cushions. I left them on your bed."

Kate nodded her thanks and walked down the hall to her bedroom. She picked up the letters and read the front of the envelope. One was addressed to her and one to Mary. Kate's heartbeat sped up. She dropped the envelope for Mary back on the bed and took hers to the bathroom with her. She started her bath, making sure the water was hot and fragrant.

When the water was ready, she sank down into the water and sighed. She rested her head against the pillow and closed her eyes. Letting her mind wander where it wanted. Memories of Brad and their life played through her mind and abruptly, she remembered the letter. She reached for it and opened the envelope. Pulling the letter out, she tossed the envelope aside. Her heart racing, she opened the letter.

Dear Kate,

I don't even know how to start this letter. I miss you so much it hurts. I am so sorry for all the pain I've caused you. Please believe me when I tell you it was better this way and I was only thinking of you and Mary.

I was diagnosed with cancer a week after we learned you were pregnant with Mary. It was already Stage 4 and nothing could have been done. It was a death sentence. I knew you'd fight, tooth and nail, for my life. And I couldn't let you do that. I couldn't let you waste the energy and time...when it would be all for nothing anyway. The doctor gave me a year to live.

At first, I thought I could keep it from you and we could go on and live our lives until mine ended. You loved me so much and I you. I was falling fast in love with our baby and I hadn't even met her yet. I knew that if I stayed, I'd never be able to leave. And I knew you'd eventually find out and make me fight. And I couldn't let you do that, either. I didn't want to jeopardize Mary's well-being with the stress of treatments and care that would ultimately have fallen on you. And then once she came, to have her mother's attention so divided, it wouldn't have been fair.

It broke my heart to see the pain I caused you. I would hear you cry yourself to sleep at night and that's when I started sleeping at the office. I had to stay away or I'd confess everything. The day you left, it was the worst day of my life, but I knew it was for the best. You had to believe it was completely over, that I didn't care you were leaving. And that was the day my life ended for me. All I had to do was wait it out, wait for you to file for divorce.

I am so sorry for everything. Know that if it had been possible, I would have been with you until we were old and gray. I'll love you forever.

Brad

Kate pressed a kiss to the letter. She had her answers, but they didn't bring her the closure she thought they would. Brad had been right. She would have fought for his life as he'd fought for hers. Their future had been so bright. She could imagine his devastation when he learned of the cancer. An abrupt end to a beautiful life. And now she understood his coldness. He'd been protecting her and Mary.

As Kate went to put the letter back in the envelope, she noticed more papers inside. She found a copy of Brad's will and fresh tears rolled down her face. As she scanned the document, she realized that Brad had kept her as his beneficiary. And her jaw dropped when she realized that he'd cashed in his life insurance policy and set up an account for her. At the bottom of the letter was a quick, handwritten note.

Kate, I didn't really get rid of everything. I moved it into a storage unit. The code is our wedding anniversary. The house is all yours too, if you want it. All my love, Brad.

Kate dropped the letters and envelope onto the floor and sobbed. Would the pain never end? She'd found the perfect man, husband and father and now he was gone. Life would never be the same. She'd never be the same.

As her tears subsided, she splashed her face with water. Kate leaned back onto the bath pillow and closing her eyes, she did the only thing she could think of, something she hadn't done in a really long time. She prayed. She thanked God for the precious time she'd had with Brad. She thanked God for bringing him into her life. To keep his soul safe and loved until she could join him in eternity. And she asked for peace and healing for herself and Mary. They had a long road ahead and she knew she'd never get through it without His help, love and guidance.

Chapter Nine

Kate sighed a little as she glanced out the plane window. They were close to Heathrow airport and she expected to hear the announcement of their imminent arrival any minute.

The past five years had been hard. Losing Brad had torn a hole in her soul. She had patched it up as best she could with group therapy and going to church. But Mary had been what kept her going those first months, and was what kept her patched even now. Mary was the light her life and she shuddered to think what life would be like without Mary.

Georgie and Erin had been suggesting lately that she needed to get out there and meet someone. She'd been able to fend off their attempts at matchmaking so far, but it would only be a matter of time before they trapped her.

Kate wasn't sure if she was ready to meet anyone new. When she'd married Brad, she had envisioned it for life. Even when she'd served him with divorce papers, she still had held out hope he'd change his mind and want them back. His death had changed everything. Some days, she would wake up and forget for a split second that he was gone and when the memories came crashing down, the pain would feel fresh and new.

Those days were fewer and further between now, but she

was still unsure. It was a big step. But what made her consider it at times wasn't Georgie and Erin's interference. It was the way Mary would sometimes watch a father and daughter play in the park. Or when she'd come home from daycare and talk about all the fathers that picked up their children.

Kate wasn't going to lie. She missed the intimacy of a husband. She missed sharing a bed, sharing the shower for some early morning fun. Sharing meals and inside jokes. She missed having someone there to reach the items on the top shelf. Or someone to help bring in the groceries. Someone to snuggle on the couch with. Someone to talk to and share the day with. And she knew Mary was missing out too.

Kate sighed again and closed her eyes. The only way to deal with it would be to let fate take the reins. Going out and forcing the issue wasn't how it worked for Kate. Fate had brought Brad into Kate's life. She was content to let fate bring someone new into her life. And if it never happened, Kate would accept that.

"Good afternoon ladies and gentlemen, this is your captain speaking. We will be landing in about twenty minutes. Please return to your seats and fasten your seat belts. We know you have a choice when it comes to air travel. Thank you for choosing British Airways."

Kate watched as the flight attendants snapped to action. They came around to take last minute trash, made sure the seats were upright and tray tables were stowed. Kate took out her compact and checked her appearance. She quickly dusted her nose with powder, reapplied her lipstick and fluffed her hair. She replaced her makeup bag in her purse and put it under the seat in front of her.

The captain touched down with barely a bump. Kate appreciated his smooth landing. It was the one part of flying that always unnerved her. The taxi to the gate was short. Too quickly they were parked and it was time to fight the masses to get her bags and get off the plane...all in one piece. She'd done this trip so many times in the past five years and she understood the mad dash. They'd been on the plane for eight long hours, everyone was ready to stretch their legs and breathe in fresh air. Kate kept her seat until most of the people had deplaned.

She caught a cab and headed to the hotel in Mayfair, The Washington Mayfair Hotel. Kate loved this hotel. It was so elegant, posh and beautiful. This was definitely one of the more fabulous perks of working where she did. How often did you find a position that allowed you to travel to one of the world's greatest cities, work for part of the day and then be free to sight-see and enjoy the city? She thanked God everyday for this position.

Kate checked in to her room and quickly went upstairs to unpack. She'd arrived two days late because she'd had to get Mary registered for Kindergarten. Kate couldn't believe it was time for kindergarten, the time had flown by. She certainly wasn't ready to watch Mary take this next step. Pretty soon she'd be graduating from high school, heading off to college, getting a job and getting married. Pushing these bittersweet thoughts out of her mind before she broke down in tears, Kate headed out to find Erin.

Kate wandered in to the hotel pub, hoping Erin would be there. Kate enjoyed the hotel pub, the atmosphere was cheery and she always felt at home inside. Not finding Erin in the pub, Kate wandered back out and strolled along the street, stopping to peer into shop windows and enjoy the alone time. She loved Mary fiercely, but Kate was able to admit to herself that having a break every few months was good not only for her own well-being but also for her relationship with Mary.

As Kate wandered the streets of Mayfair, she reveled in the lovely warm air. She enjoyed walking in London. She loved the hustle and bustle of the the more commercial areas and she loved the quiet streets of the residential areas. She'd read somewhere about a man named Samuel Johnson who in 1777 said, *'When a man is tired of London, he is tired of life; for there is in London all that life can afford.'* The more time Kate spent in London, the more she could understand what he meant. There really was so much to do here. Museums, theater, food, sports, parks, castles and so much more. Kate figured it would take her at least a lifetime to get through all the things she wanted to see.

Realizing she was hungry, Kate decided to end her search for Erin and she returned to the hotel pub for dinner.

The rest of the week flew by and before she knew it, Friday had arrived. She and Erin finished up early and Erin was planning to spend the evening in her room catching up on emails and skyping with her family.

The week had been so busy, that Kate hadn't gotten a chance to eat at her favorite restaurant. Kate grabbed her purse and quickly walked out of the hotel. Pappagallo's was a warm, intimate little Italian place. Kate picked up her pace, eager to eat some dinner. As she neared the end of Curzon Street, she looked around in confusion. How had she missed it? She turned around and kept her eyes open.

She finally found where Pappagallo's used to be, but in it's place was a restaurant called Tempo. Starving, Kate shrugged and walked in. It was no longer the dim, intimate restaurant Kate remembered. Now it was a classy, upscale place, with a lot of light. The walls had very little artwork hanging on them and the tables were lined up in twos. The tables were glass and iron and were set with fine china and crystal glassware. To give the tables some color, the chairs were a turquoise suede. The salt and pepper mills were the only thing on the tables that even hinted at Italian cuisine. This did not look promising.

"May I help you?" The hostess asked.

"Uh, yes. I'd like a table please," Kate said.

"Do you have a reservation?"

"No, I don't. Do I need one?"

"Well, it is recommended, however we aren't incredibly busy yet this evening."

"It's just me," Kate smiled. "I'm sorry, but I'm so curious. Can you tell me what happened to Pappagallo's?"

"They closed about three months ago. My husband and I bought the restaurant and gave it a facelift. My husband is the chef."

Standing in front of her was a woman of Japanese descent. Her black hair fell straight down her back. Her almond shaped eyes were wide-spaced and a deep chocolate brown. Her cheekbones were angled sharply and she had a beauty mark at the corner of her right eye. She wore the traditional Japanese kimono, and Kate wondered what she'd gotten herself into. "Do you serve Japanese cuisine?"

The hostess smiled. "Not entirely. We serve Italian food with a Japanese flair. Would you care to follow me to your table?"

"Yes, why not," Kate shrugged again. She was starving and willing to give the place a chance.

"Enjoy your meal," the hostess told her.

Kate placed her napkin in her lap and looked around. She had to admit that the light coming through the windows was beautiful. It made the crystal on the tables shimmer, casting a million rainbows all over the room.

"Hello ma'am! Welcome to Tempo! My name is Ricardo and I'll be your server this evening. Here is our menu for this evening. Our chef is preparing a roasted organic salmon with monk's beard and salsa verde. Pan-fried scallops with golden beetroot, lemon and chili. And finally we have roasted duck breast with wild garlic mash, green kale, blood orange and red wine. May I get you something to drink?"

"Yes, please. I'd like a chilled chardonnay and an ice water, no lemon."

"I'll get those for you right away. Would you care for a moment to review our menu?"

"Please," Kate said. She watched the waiter walk away and was surprised at how eager and excited he was about the restaurant, the menu and it seemed, even his job. They must pay well, or he gets incredible tips!

Kate looked over the menu and sighed a sad sigh. None of the menu items were traditional Italian dishes. She was really craving a hearty lasagna but she didn't even see that option on the menu. Looking each option over carefully, Kate finally settled on Cappesante. They were pan-fried scallops married with golden beetroot, lemon and chili. Scallops were her favorite seafood, she was curious to see how this restaurant would prepare them.

While she waited for Ricardo to return, Kate gazed around the restaurant. There were a few couples in the restaurant and Kate wondered if they had ever dined at Pappagallo's and like her were trying out this new place. She was willing to try this new restaurant, but she missed Pappagallo's. She wondered what happened to Mama Maria and Papa Don. She hoped they were okay.

"Here we are ma'am," Ricardo said as he placed her drinks on the table. "Have you decided what you'd like?"

"Yes. I'd like the Cappesante, please. I'd also like an order of the roast potatoes."

"Certainly. If there's anything else you need, just let me know."

"Actually, I do have a question. Do you happen to know anything about the owners of Pappagallo's? Where they might be, what they might be doing?"

Ricardo's face fell and Kate felt her heart clutch. "Papa Don died a few months ago and Mama Maria couldn't bear the thought of keeping the restaurant open. When she took Papa Don back to Italy, she stayed. It's been hard on her, they were childhood sweethearts."

"Oh my, that's so sad. You wouldn't happen to have an address for her, would you?"

"I do. I keep in touch with her. I don't have it with me today, but if you stop by tomorrow, I'll bring it for you."

"I'm leaving in the morning. Do you mind if I call here tomorrow when I get home?"

"Sure. I'm here by four."

"Thank you. I only visit London a couple of times a year, but I always made it a point to go in there. Papa Don was a genius. I'll miss him."

"He was indeed. I worked for them for many years, they were both such wonderful people. They are quite missed here in the neighborhood."

"I imagine they are. I didn't know them well, but Mama Maria always remembered me when I would come in. She is so special. Thank you for telling me."

She watched him walk away with a heavy heart. Poor Mama Maria. She remembered many conversations she'd had with Mama Maria about their life, how'd they met, where they'd been and all they'd done together. Papa Don had meant the world to Mama Maria. She couldn't even imagine being with someone for so long and then losing them. She'd known her own loss, and the pain from that still took her breath away. It must be a hundred times worse for Mama Maria.

"Excuse me."

Startled, Kate looked up into a pair of the most gorgeous blue eyes she'd ever seen. "Y-Yes?" She stammered.

"I was sitting across the way there and I couldn't help but overhear your conversation with Ricardo. You knew Mama Maria?"

He'd been sitting across the way and she'd overlooked him? "Yes, but not well. I always stop into Pappagallo's when I'm in town. I was surprised to see it closed. And in fact, I got a bit lost trying to find it," Kate smiled.

"Do you mind if I sit?" The man asked, gesturing toward her empty chair.

"Um, no." Kate looked around to see if anyone else was having trouble believing this man was actually joining her. No one else seemed to be paying them any mind.

As he sat down, Kate studied his face. His nose was long and aquiline and he had a full lush mouth. His face was square and he had a small dent in his chin. His hair was wavy falling to his collar with a chunk that fell over his eye. The man was absolutely gorgeous.

"Thank you. I'm sure you're wondering what I'm doing," he grinned at her.

"Um, well...now that you mention it," Kate smiled.

"Pappagallo's was my favorite restaurant. I grew up in Mayfair and worked for them for many years when I was a lad. They were a staple in Mayfair. I love to talk to people who also appreciated them. It brings back so many wonderful memories."

"Oh, I'm so sorry. It must be hard for you to come back and not have them around," Kate said gently.

"I travel a lot and am gone for weeks, sometimes months at a time. I feel fortunate that I was here when Papa Don died. Mama Maria was in no shape to handle any of the arrangements. I still have trouble walking down Curzon and not seeing the bright red awning."

Kate laughed. "Yes! That's why I was lost, I couldn't find the awning."

He smiled. "Yoshi has done a fantastic job with Tempo and I promise, you'll enjoy the food immensely."

"Why do you travel so much, what do you do?"

"I'm in entertainment," he said after a brief hesitation.

"Really? That must be exciting!"

The man laughed. "Yes, sometimes it is and at other times it's frustrating."

"Oh yes, I know what you mean. I think all jobs, no matter how much you love them, can be labors of love and banes of existence." Kate paused and held out her hand. "I'm Kate."

He gripped her hand firmly. "My name is Edward."

"Nice to meet you." Kate took a sip of her wine. "So you said you're gone for weeks and months at a time. Will you be leaving again soon?"

"No, I actually just got back yesterday. I'm planning to be here for a month or so. Are you in town for long?"

Kate laughed, "I wish! I'm leaving tomorrow. My employer has an office here and we visit quarterly for a week. I love it here so much that if my whole world weren't back in the U.S., I'd probably move here."

"London does get into your blood. I've heard many Americans say that. What is it about London that you like so much?"

Kate sat back in her chair, sipped her wine, and took him through the London she loved. From the Tower of London and all it's history to the beautiful parks that dotted London to the dinner cruises down the River Thames. The people, the shopping, the food – which left a lot to be desired in most cases.

"It's fascinating," Edward said. "Don't you Americans have this stuff in the U.S.?"

"Oh, of course we do. We have Broadway, we have parks, we have shopping. But the history that's here, it oozes out of everything in London. Everyone of you live and breathe it everyday. I think it's wonderful."

Ricardo returned with her dinner. "Here you are, ma'am. Would you care for another glass of wine?"

"I would, thank you."

Ricardo disappeared to get her wine.

"I'll let you eat. It was so nice talking with you," Edward said as he started to rise.

"Oh please, stay," Kate surprised herself by saying. "Keep me company while I eat, unless you have someplace to be?" *Were these words really coming from her mouth?*

"I don't have anywhere I'd rather be at the moment," he said smiling as he pulled his chair closer to the table. When Ricardo came back, Edward asked for a glass of Pinot Noir.

"Where are some of the more exotic places you've been?" Kate cut a scallop in half and speared it with her fork. Dunking it into the salsa verde, she popped it in her mouth. Kate closed her eyes and concentrated on the flavors currently assaulting her tongue. It was delectable. The lemon and chili warred for attention and the scallop was tender and juicy. The salsa verde gave it just the right kick and melded perfectly with the lemon, chili and beetroot.

Opening her eyes, she was startled to see Edward staring at her. He smiled making the laugh lines around his eyes visible and led her to think that this was a man who laughed often. "It's good, isn't it?"

Kate shook her head. "No, it's not good. It's amazing. Superb. I've never tasted scallops so tender and juicy. It's delicious and I see what you mean," Kate smiled.

"Yes, Yoshi is brilliant. Would you like to meet him?"

Kate goggled at Edward. "Meet him? I thought they were like Gods and no mere mortals could be near them?"

Edward laughed. "You're wonderful!"

Kate joined in his laughter. "It feels good to laugh," Kate said as she wiped a tear from her eye. She picked up her fork and enjoyed more of her dinner.

"Yoshi can be temperamental, but he enjoys meeting his customers. Especially the ones who think he's a God."

Kate laughed. "This really is the best meal I've had in a long time. Papa Don's food was comfort. This is art."

"Ah, yes. Yoshi would definitely want to meet you."

"And I'd be happy to meet him, later." Kate took another bite and sighed. "So, you were going to tell me all the fun and interesting places you've been on your travels."

"Right. Where should I start?"

"At the beginning. Tell me of the very first place you visited."

"That's easy. Scotland. My mother has family there. Her sister and some cousins. We would travel up during the summer, which made me angry when I got older and knew what I was missing here in London. But it never failed, we'd go up for six weeks in the summer and sometimes we'd go up in the winter if my aunt was popping out another baby. My mother liked to go up and 'help'." Edward said as he used air quotes for help.

"How many children does your aunt have?"

"Ten."

"Ten?!? Oh my! She's brave!" Kate laughed.

"Brave is a word for it," Edward laughed. "Of course they're all grown now and living their lives. They're good kids though, they remember their mother and are always helping her with whatever she needs. And they fill in for me with my own mother when I travel."

"Oh that's nice. You don't find too much of that anymore. Most of the people I know are too concerned with themselves to do anything for anyone else."

"That's very cynical, but true," Edward agreed. "Is London the only place you've been?"

"Yes. Until I was offered this job, I'd never traveled outside of the U.S." Finished with her dinner, Kate sighed and pushed her plate away. She took another sip of her wine. "Didn't know what I was missing."

"And you still don't. London is just a small part of the world. Where else would you like to see?"

"Japan, Australia, Italy. The Caribbean. Mexico. Alaska. Hollywood. Hawaii," Kate shrugged. "I know those last few are in America, but I'd still like to see them."

Ricardo arrived and swept her plate up. "Dessert for you?"

Kate patted her stomach. "Oh, I don't know. I had thought about the pear and almond tart, but I think I'm too full now."

"Ricardo, bring us the tart – I'll help her eat it. Kate, would you like some coffee?"

"Actually, tea, please. And thank you! That tart sounds good and I really didn't want to miss out on it," Kate smiled.

"Tea for Kate, and I'd like a large espresso, please."

"Right away, sir."

"Tell me, Edward. Why don't you have something more important or fun to do than to sit here with me, a stranger, and watch me eat my dinner?"

"I suppose you'll think me odd, but I enjoy doing my own thing. Usually I'm at the beck and call of others and when I'm home I like doing what I want, when I want."

"That's not odd, that's normal. That's how I am when I'm here. Other than during the day when I'm helping Erin with work. The afternoon and evenings are my own time. It's nice to have that down time with no responsibilities. Come and go as you please. Enjoying yourself and the surroundings. It's so freeing." Kate took a sip of her water.

"It is. It's too bad you're leaving tomorrow. I'd really like to spend more time with you."

Kate coughed on her water. "Y-You would?"

"I would," Edward paused and studied her face. "That surprises you?"

"Y-Yes, a little. You've only just met me."

"How else does one get to know another person?"

"But I'm not from here," Kate said.

Edward laughed. "Are you afraid?"

"Afraid of what?"

"Of getting to know me?"

"Not exactly. I mean, you seem nice and you're interesting. I've enjoyed our conversation a lot," Kate started.

"But you live on the other side of the ocean and you have no idea how to keep a chance meeting growing into something bigger."

"Exactly. I just don't know what else to say. I'm leaving tomorrow. Maybe fate will look favorably on us again and we'll run into each other the next time I'm in town," Kate said.

She was relieved when Ricardo stopped at their table with the pear almond tart and their drinks. He cleared away the wine glasses. "Anything else I can bring you?"

"Just the check please," Kate said. "Thank you, Ricardo."

Kate took a sip of her tea and then cut a piece of the tart. She placed it on her tongue and again was blown away. It was divine. "This is delicious," Kate whispered.

"Why are you whispering?"

"Because I don't want to ruin the experience," Kate whispered.

"I understand." Edward took a bite of the tart.

They continued to chitchat throughout dessert and Kate was relieved when the previous topic didn't come up again. Ricardo returned with the check and Edward snatched it up before Kate could even flinch. "Edward!" Kate exclaimed as she reached for the check. "Please, you don't have to do that."

"I know, but it's my pleasure. I intruded on your time and enjoyed myself thoroughly. It's the least I can do."

"Thank you," Kate said sincerely. She took another sip of her tea and wondered about the man sitting across from her. He dressed nicely, Kate could tell they were designer clothes. His manners were impeccable. He seemed well-educated and had told her of his travels. He was handsome, more than handsome. She liked the way his eyes twinkled when he smiled. She liked the way he stared at her, as if she was a work of art that was hanging in the gallery. She could see herself spending time with him and enjoying his company.

"You're welcome," Edward said.

Kate smiled. She rose to leave and watched in awe as Edward rose with her. *He definitely has good manners*, Kate thought. Kate stuck out her hand, "It was such a pleasure to meet you, Edward."

Edward took her hand firmly in his and lifted it to his lips. "The pleasure was mine," Edward murmured against her hand. "Until we meet again."

"Goodbye," Kate murmured and she could feel her cheeks warming. She'd never met anyone like Edward and she wondered as she left the restaurant, if they would ever meet again.

Chapter Ten

Three months later...

Kate was exhausted. Mary had been up practically every hour the night before with a fever. When her fever had risen to 103, Kate had panicked and taken Mary to the emergency room. Kate could count on one hand the number of times Mary'd had a fever, let alone be sick, in her life. She counted herself lucky that Mary hadn't been one to catch every virus and bug that she came in contact with. Kate had heard stories of the kids with constant stomach viruses, colds or the dreaded ear infections.

After spending three hours at the ER, the doctors hadn't found anything wrong with Mary, concluding it was just a virus that must be going around. Georgie had insisted that Kate not cancel her trip to London. A fever wasn't enough to keep her and Tim from getting their week with Mary.

As the taxi pulled up to the hotel, Kate envisioned the pampering she was about to indulge in. She'd brought the new Anita Blake book and was planning to order some wine and sink into a hot bath with lots of fragrant bubbles.

"Welcome back, Ms. Walker," the front desk attendant greeted.

"Thank you," Kate said. "Has Ms. McNamara arrived yet?"

"Let me check on that for you, one second." She tapped a few keys on the computer, looked up and smiled. "It looks like Ms. McNamara has not arrived yet. Would you like to leave a message for her?"

"If you could just tell her that I'm here, but going to bed, I would appreciate it. I'll see her at breakfast in the morning."

"My pleasure, Ms. Walker." She tapped a few more keys and began Kate's checking in process. "It seems you have a message," the attendant said as she passed Kate a slip of paper.

"It's probably from Ms. McNamara," Kate said as she slipped it into her pocket.

The attendant pushed a form across the counter. "Please sign on the line. I'll just swipe your card for incidentals while you're doing that."

Used to the routine of checking in, Kate was already prepared with her credit card resting on the counter. She signed the form and passed it back to the attendant.

"Here's your card, Ms. Walker. Can I help you with anything else before you head upstairs?"

"No, thank you. I'm all set."

The attendant passed Kate her room key. "Enjoy your stay."

Kate hefted her bags and quickly walked to the elevators. When she got to her room, she opened the door and deposited her bags on the bed. She walked over to the phone and called down to room service, ordering chilled white wine and a fruit and cheese platter. The light dinner would suffice as she planned to make it an early night.

She walked into the bathroom, started the water for her bath and then put her things in order while she waited for room service to arrive. When she pulled her suits out of the suitcase, she was relieved to see that they'd made the trip with minimal damage. A quick iron in the morning would be all she had to do to make herself presentable.

Just as she finished putting her things away, she heard a knock at the door. "Yum, wine," Kate murmured to herself as she crossed the room to answer the door. She signed the slip and deposited the order on the desk. Pouring herself a large glass of wine, she gathered up her robe and book and retreated to the bathroom.

Sinking into the bubbles, Kate sighed with contentment. It felt decadent to be able to drink wine and soak away her stresses in the tub. She wouldn't trade her life for any amount of money, but these little breaks were so good for her soul.

She took a sip of her wine and cracked open the latest installment of Anita Blake. Unashamed of her complete obsession with these books, Kate couldn't wait to continue reading about Anita and Jean Claude's adventures. There was no doubt in her mind that Anita was meant to be with Jean Claude. She didn't argue that he was powerful and would do whatever he had to in order to survive, but he adored Anita. Kate thought their love story was timeless and at times she could admit she longed for a love story of her own. She was lonely and while her life was beyond busy, she felt that she was meant to find love again. Or at least she hoped she was.

I wonder if I'll bump into Edward? She thought to herself. Smiling, she took another sip of wine. She didn't think it was likely as it had been a chance meeting to begin with. And if she remembered correctly, he traveled a lot for his job. But oh, he was hot and she definitely wouldn't be opposed to bumping into him on this trip.

Putting him out of her mind, she sipped more wine and began her book. Two hours later, water chilly and her wine long since gone, Kate emerged from her bath. Quickly toweling herself dry, she wrapped herself in a robe and refilled her wine glass. Climbing into her warm bed, she sipped more wine and continued reading her book. She was completely hooked and the early night she'd planned on was out the window.

When she started to nod off, Kate reluctantly put aside her book and went into the bathroom to get ready for bed. After finishing her beauty routine, Kate went back into the room to hang up her clothes. As she was folding her pants, the slip of paper the front desk attendant had given her fell out of the pocket. Picking it up, she gave a slight gasp when she unfolded the note and began to read.

Kate,
I thoroughly enjoyed meeting you last night and I hope the next time you're in town, you'll give me a call. I promise I'm not a crazy stalker, even though this note probably paints me as such. My number is below.
    —Edward

Kate giggled and refolded the note. She'd love to see him, but it had been three months, surely he'd forgotten about the note and her. He seemed a very sophisticated, well-traveled and busy man.

No, Kate would leave it up to fate one more time. Fate had served them well once before. Maybe if they didn't find each other this trip, she'd give him a call the next time, after all, three months was a long time.

She thought back to that dinner at Tempo and how much she'd enjoyed the food and the man.

The following morning, after her dinner with Edward, she'd shared a taxi with Erin to the airport. Kate remembered she had been staring out the window, watching the passing scenery, when Erin had nudged her.

"You okay, Kate? Where's your 'Mary Smile'?" Erin asked.

Smiling, Kate glanced up at Erin. "I'm happy to get home and see Mary."

"But?" Erin asked.

"But I found out that Papa Don died a couple of months ago."

"What?! That's horrible." Erin interrupted.

Kate nodded. "Mama Maria took him back to Italy for the funeral and ended up staying there with her family. She sold the business and a Japanese couple bought it. It's now called Tempo. Since I was already there, I decided to try it. The food was amazing!"

"Really? I didn't think you liked Japanese food," Erin quizzed.

"I don't, but this chef melds the Japanese and Italian. And I gotta say, it works." Kate paused, sadness washing over her as she thought of Mama Maria. "I told my waiter I'd call him when I got home for Mama's address in Italy. I really want to send her a card."

"Pass it to me as well, please. I didn't know them as well as you did, but I'd also like to send something."

"I will," Pausing again, Kate wondered if she should mention her encounter with Edward. "The strangest thing happened last night. While I was asking the waiter for information about Mama Maria, this incredibly handsome man joined me. Apparently he used to work at Pappagallo's a long time ago, and said he liked hearing stories about them because it brought back good memories. We ended up chatting through dinner," Kate grinned.

A smile lit up Erin's face. "You have got to be kidding me! That's great, Kate! How handsome is incredibly handsome?"

"Beyond incredibly," Kate smirked.

"Sooo...are you going to see him again? Are you ready for something like this? Maybe I'm thinking too far ahead, but I'm just curious. This is what, the first man since Brad that you've even shown an ounce of interest in?"

"I'm not sure. I've been asking myself that same question. We had such a nice time and I really enjoyed his company. He's been to so many places, he said he was in the entertainment industry. He seems well-educated, he dressed very nicely and he had impressive manners.   We didn't exchange any information. It was a chance meeting. Besides, I live in the U.S. and he lives here, for the most part. I can't imagine anything will really come of it." Kate said.

If she'd known then that Edward had been just as affected by their chance meeting as she had, she might very well have exchanged phone numbers or email addresses with him before she left London the last time.

Sighing with pleasure from Edward's note and the memories of that dinner, Kate turned off the light and snuggled down into the covers. She was asleep moments after her head hit the pillow.

Chapter Eleven

Kate woke the next day with a smile on her face. She was still glowing from the note she'd received and after sleeping on it, was still sure she wanted to leave a second meeting to fate.

Kate was just about to leave her room and head down to breakfast, when the phone rang. Kate hurried over to it and answered. "This is Kate."

"Kate, it's Erin." Tears in her voice, Erin continued. "I'm sorry I didn't call last night, it's been touch and go here all night."

Kate sat down on her bed and gripped the phone tightly. "Erin, what's wrong? What's happened?"

Her voice breaking, Erin explained. "It's Lily, she was hit by a car yesterday. Oh my God, Kate. Her heart has stopped twice and she's in a coma right now. Luke and I haven't left her side."

"Oh Erin, oh my God, I'm so so sorry. What can I do?"

"There's nothing to be done right now. We just have to wait," Erin replied in a strangled voice.

"Erin, are you sure? I can be on the next plane."

"I'm sure. I need you there, we have so much to accomplish this week. I feel good knowing you're there," Erin said. She paused a moment to get her voice under control. "Kate, my baby."

"What happened?"

"I don't really know. Luke said she got off the bus and was walking up the driveway. Sophie started crying, so Luke turned from the door to soothe her. The next thing he knows, brakes are screeching and Lily's lying in the street. We don't know if she saw something, someone or what happened. The driver was this little old woman and she was hysterical. The paramedics had to give her something to get her to calm down."

"Was she able to tell you what happened?"

"No, she was too hysterical and when they finally got her calmed down, she went into shock and wasn't able to talk. Oh God, Kate. I have chills, I can't catch my breath. I don't know how to feel or what to do."

"Talk to her, Erin. Let her hear your voice. Hold her hand and pray. That's all you can do. I'll be praying all day for you."

Kate continued to talk to Erin until she was called away by her husband. "Don't worry about anything here, Erin. I've got this covered. Focus all of yourself on Lily and your family."

"Thank you, Kate. I'll keep you updated."

The day flew by, which surprised Kate. As worried as she was for Erin's daughter, Lily, there was so much to do to get the new product lines launched. Kate had been in meetings most of the day with the suppliers and the retailers. Working out the details of everything and trying to make everyone happy was very difficult. She had new admiration and respect for Erin. Erin made it look so easy, but after today, Kate understood why Erin was plagued with headaches at each product launch.

Leaving the office well after eight that night, Kate decided to order up room service and check to see if there was an update waiting for her from Erin on Lily's condition. Kate had paused several times throughout the day to offer up a prayer of healing for Lily and peace for Erin and Luke.

The next morning, Kate woke early to the phone ringing. Fumbling around for the receiver, Kate managed to knock her cell phone and book off the nightstand before finally grabbing the receiver and putting it to her ear.

"Hello?" Kate answered.

"Kate, it's Erin."

Sitting up, Kate turned on the lamp beside the bed. "Erin! Is Lily okay?"

"She's awake!"

"Oh, thank God! Erin, that's wonderful!"

"She woke up a couple of hours ago. She asked for some water and told us that she hurt," Erin snorted. "We haven't asked her what happened, she's still pretty out of it."

"How are you and Luke holding up? What do the doctors have to say?"

"The doctors are saying it's good news that she's awake and talking to us. She recognized us immediately and knew the answers to all those memory questions they ask. They'll do some more scans soon to ensure all is okay inside her head and that there's no surprise internal bleeding."

"I'm so happy that she's pulled through. I can't even imagine how you and Luke must be holding up."

"We're doing okay. Before she woke up, I wanted to throw a temper tantrum and throw blame everywhere. But I can't. I know how Lily and Sophie operate, they move so fast-"

"All kids do, any parent can tell you that," Kate interrupted.

"Right. And poor Luke, he's devastated."

"Don't let him beat himself up over this, Erin. You know he will," Kate said.

"Yeah, I've been trying to talk him down from that ledge," Erin's voice broke. "But I know if I was in his place, I'd be doing the same thing."

"What can I do, how can I help?"

"Doing what you're doing. You're such a good friend," Erin said gratefully.

"I wish I was there with you," Kate said softly. "I know that I'm doing good here and that you need me here since you can't be. But you're my friend and I feel as if my place should be right next to you."

"Thank you," Erin said. "I want you here too, but I need you there."

"And here I'll stay," Kate said with a small smile. "Keep me updated and please, call when you get the results from the tests."

"I will. I'll talk to you soon."

"Take care of yourself and each other," Kate said.

For the second day in a row, the day flew by. She spent most of the day working with the designers to get the designs finalized and a schedule made for samples of the designs to be made. As she left the office and stepped outside, she took several deep breaths of fresh air and could feel some of the stress dissipate. Deciding a brisk walk would further help alleviate her stress, she took off down the street in the direction of the only restaurant she could dream of going to, Tempo.

As soon as Kate walked in the door, the hostess and chef's wife, Joni, hurried over to greet her. "Kate, you're back! How lovely to see you," she said as she kissed Kate's cheek.

"Hello, Joni! How are you?" Kate returned the cheek busses and gave her a hug.

"Oh, we're doing well. We've been so busy lately, it's tiring but great!" Joni said excitedly.

"That makes me happy. I don't know where I'd eat if you guys closed down shop!" Kate said laughing.

"Come, let me show you to your table. Ricardo is off tonight, but he did tell me to say 'Hello' if I saw you. Consider yourself told," Joni said as she placed the menu in front of Kate.

Kate laughed. "Thank you for the message. Please, tell him I also said 'Hello'. And that I was disappointed that he wasn't here," she said.

"Enjoy your dinner, Kate!"

Kate smiled to herself as she picked up her menu.

"May I join you?"

Kate's head whipped up and her jaw dropped. "Edward, hello!" While she had hoped that fate would favor them again, she hadn't really believed it would. Smiling broadly and giving fate a high five in her mind, Kate gestured toward the chair opposite her. "Yes, please!"

"How are you, Kate?"

"Better now that you're here," Kate smiled. "Yourself?"

"Sending my heartfelt gratitude to fate," Edward laughed.

"As am I," Kate laughed.

"Have you been in town, long?" Edward asked.

"Two days. We've been crazy busy at work, this is the first night I've had the energy to get out of the hotel."

"When do you go back to the States?"

"Saturday morning," Kate replied. "Have you already eaten dinner?"

"No, I haven't been here long. Just enough time to order a glass of wine and begin perusing the menu."

Kate smiled and looked over her own menu. Everything sounded delicious, and she decided to go with the gressingham duck paired with parmesan and pistachio. She chose chilled white wine to drink. Edward selected the ravioli which was made with dorset crab, prawns, basil and lime.

After giving their orders and passing the menus to the server, Kate focused her attention on her dinner companion. She was thanking her lucky stars for the chance to meet Edward again.

As they continued to talk and learn about each other, Kate was amazed at the ease with which they were able to converse. She felt as comfortable with Edward as she did with any one of her friends. He was a good listener and very easy to talk to. They discussed her busy days at work and his travel schedule. He entertained her with stories of some of the pranks he played on his sisters when they were younger. He told her of his latest trip to Austria for work. He never went into detail about what he specifically did, but Kate didn't really notice the exclusion. She was charmed and entertained and perfectly content to sit in this tiny restaurant with this handsome man.

After sharing a very scrumptious dessert of bavarese, poached pear filled with ricotta cheese and gently drizzled with blood orange syrup, Kate leaned back in her chair and sipped her tea. "That was delicious. I'm kind of glad I don't live here, I'd eat in this restaurant every night and end up gaining fifty pounds!"

Edward laughed, "I doubt that very much." Taking a sip of his coffee, he glanced into Kate's eyes. "Do you have plans tomorrow night?"

"Not really. I would like to visit the aquarium and the London Eye this week, but I don't have anything specifically planned. With work so crazy, I'm not sure I'll be able to do any sight-seeing this week, anyway."

"Would you care to join me on a driving tour of the countryside?"

"I don't know. I mean, it sounds lovely and all," Kate hedged.

"But we're still just strangers, right?"

Laughing, Kate nodded. "I'm sorry. That must be incredibly insulting to hear."

Edward shook his head. "Not at all. How about we meet for dinner again?"

"I would like that." Kate's smile was bright as she gazed into Edward's eyes. "Very much."

"Excellent. Shall we meet at the Mews tomorrow night at seven?"

"Absolutely," Kate agreed.

"Let me give you my number in case you get held up," Edward said.

Kate laughed. "It's ok, I think I have it. You left me a note at the front desk and it included your number," Kate explained at Edward's quizzical glance.

"You got it! Brilliant, I wasn't sure if they'd kept it all this time." Edward grinned. "I'm glad that didn't scare you off."

"Not at all. It made me smile," Kate rose and gathered her things. Edward took her coat from her and helped her into it. When was the last time someone helped her into her coat? Kate sighed with pleasure. It was these small things that she missed.

He was going to be trouble for her heart and she wasn't entirely sure she was ready to put herself out there again. The past five years had been hell in some ways and Kate was only now finding her footing.

"Thank you. I'll see you tomorrow," Kate smiled and turned to leave. She thanked the hostess on her way out. Once she made it through the door, she paused and inhaled deeply. What was she doing? Her heart felt giddy and light. A feeling she hadn't experienced in so long.

Chapter Twelve

Kate awoke to the ringing of the phone again the next morning. Knowing it was Erin, Kate took an extra moment to wake up and turn on the light before she answered the phone.

"Good morning, Erin," Kate said, her voice gravelly from sleep.

"Oh, Kate, did I wake you? I'm sorry," Erin apologized.

"No worries, Erin. How's Lily?" Kate asked as she sat up in bed, pulling the covers around her to keep warm.

"Much better. She was less groggy today. The doctors reviewed the scans and haven't found any internal bleeding."

"Excellent, I'm so happy to hear that," Kate interrupted. "Thank God."

"Indeed. And thank you for all your prayers," Erin said. "How are things going in London?"

Kate gave Erin a report on what had been happening at the office. She tried not to go into deep details, wanting to spare Erin any added stress.

"It sounds like things are going well. I really appreciate you taking the helm on this project, Kate. You've really made it so I can focus on Lily and my family. You have no idea how much I appreciate that," Erin said.

"You know I'd do more if I could," Kate said.

"Yes, I do. So, what else is going on in London?"

"Guess who I bumped into last night?" Kate asked her.

"Not the incredibly handsome Edward?"

"The one and the same," Kate laughed. "I went to Tempo last night for dinner and he was in there. We ate together and made another dinner date for tonight," Kate told her.

"Are you kidding me? That's great, Kate! I'm so happy for you!" Erin told her enthusiastically.

"I have butterflies, Erin."

"Of course you do, it's been a long time." Erin paused. "Hold on a minute, Kate."

"Sure," Kate said. She could hear voices talking in the background and hoped that everything was okay.

"I've gotta go, Lily is asking for me," Erin explained.

"Give her my love. I'll talk to you soon!"

As she made her way back to the hotel that afternoon, Kate decided to splurge on a massage and facial. She stopped by the front desk to schedule it and was pleasantly surprised when they told her she could go straight back and they'd take her right away.

The spa attendant showed her to the locker room. Exchanging her clothes for the warm terry robe, Kate could feel some of the stress melt away. She should have thought of this sooner; she hadn't been taking very good care of herself lately and she made a vow to herself to change that.

Kate unpinned her hair and placed all her belongings into the locker. She pressed the bell on the wall to alert the attendant that she was ready. Kate followed her down the hall to the facial room.

"Hello, Ms. Walker. My name is Renee and I'll be your facial consultant. How are you today?" The woman asked.

"I'm well, thank you. You?"

"Very good. What are we doing to your face, today?"

"Well, I think I'd like some exfoliating, some moisturizing, maybe some eyebrow waxing and whatever else you think I need. It's been awhile since I've had one of these, so I'm sure my face needs a lot of help," Kate laughed.

"Alright, Ms. Walker. Let me clean off your makeup and then we'll take it from there."

"Sounds good," Kate agreed. She leaned back in the chair, tilted her face toward the ceiling and let her mind drift. She must have dozed off because the next thing she knew, Renee was gently shaking her shoulder. "Oh! I'm so sorry," Kate apologized.

"It's not a problem. It happens a lot. We're finished here so if you'll follow me, I'll take you down to our massage therapist."

"Fantastic. Thank you so much, Renee." Kate lightly touched her face and couldn't help but sigh at how soft it felt. Kate glanced at her hand and then peeked at her toes. When was the last time she'd gotten a manicure or a pedicure. "Excuse me, Renee?"

"Yes, Ms. Walker?"

"I'm wondering, would it be possible to add in a manicure and pedicure as well?"

"I'm sure it won't be a problem. I'll go ask the front desk and let you know," Renee assured her.

"Thank you so much. I'm sorry again for falling asleep on you, I'm probably your most boring client today!"

"No, not at all. It's even hard for me to stay awake with that music playing," Renee smiled. "It's so soothing, makes me want to fall asleep too! Enjoy your massage and I'll let you know about the manicure and pedicure." Renee turned and walked toward the front of the spa.

"Hello, Ms. Walker. I'm Bree and I'll be your massage therapist. Go ahead and remove your robe and slide under the sheets, face up. I'll be back in a couple of minutes."

Kate nodded and waited for Bree to leave. She did as she was asked and was happy to feel the sheets and massage bed were warm. It was so relaxing to be encased in the warmth.

Bree knocked and then poked her head in. "All ready?"

"Yes!"

"Okay. Let's get started. We have two scents today, Jasmine Pear and Honeysuckle Rose. Which would you prefer?"

"The honeysuckle rose, please."

"That's my favorite. What type of massage would you like?"

"A full body massage, but no deep tissue. Those always make me sore for days after."

"All right, let's get started." Bree turned on the same soothing music that Renee had had in her room.

Kate relaxed all her muscles and let her mind wander. Edward popped into her head and Kate allowed herself to relive last night's dinner. She was looking forward to this evening and had to admit to herself that she was pampering herself a bit so she'd look nice for him.

Her mind wandered to Mary and she wondered what Mary was doing. She was probably having lunch and then they'd be going outside to play. Kate reminded herself to skype Mary as soon as she got back from dinner. Not that she really needed the reminder.

Dozing again, she barely woke long enough to turn over for Bree. Her muscles were feeling nice and loose. She fell back into her semi-awake state and dreamt of Brad. He was standing at the end of a long hallway and he seemed to be beckoning her to him. But as she got closer, she could see that he was actually waving to her. She waved back and walked faster, but the faster she walked the further away he got from her. Realizing she wouldn't be able to catch up to him, she stopped and glanced up on the wall. He'd left her a note saying:

Be Happy. You'll always have my heart.
Until we meet again, Brad.

She waited for the sad to come and was surprised when it didn't. Instead she felt free, almost like she'd been waiting for his permission to be happy, to be free. And now that she had it, she wasn't quite sure what to do with it or how it made her feel.

"We're all set Ms. Walker. I hope you enjoyed your massage. Renee poked her head in a little bit ago and said that they'd be happy to do a manicure and pedicure for you whenever you're ready."

A bit disoriented, Kate smiled and thanked Bree. When Bree left the room, Kate allowed herself a moment to reflect on the dream she'd had. Had it been real? Kate shook her head. Did it even matter? Brad was gone, never coming back. She knew in her heart that Brad would want her to be happy, and that she deserved to be happy.

Was this her second chance at love? Possibly. Would she allow herself to be open and accepting? Yes. Right then, Kate made up her mind. Even if Edward was not part of her end path, he was a step toward it. That path would dissolve under her feet if she kept herself closed off to new people and new experiences.

Smiling, Kate got to her feet and put on her robe. At peace with life and herself, for the first time in a long time, she walked out to the front of the spa for her manicure and pedicure.

Chapter Thirteen

"Kate, you look lovely!" Edward greeted her as he kissed Kate's cheek.

"Thank you, Edward" Kate said pleased that he noticed. "You are quite dashing, yourself!" Kate said and then sighed, quickly becoming embarrassed for saying something not only old-fashioned, but also so clichéd. "Ugh, did I really just say that?"

"You did, and I'm flattered!" Laughing, Edward held the door for Kate and ushered her into the restaurant. "I took the liberty of arriving a few minutes early and getting our table situated. I hope you don't mind."

"Not at all," Kate said as she sat down. They had a table by the window and Kate glanced outside. People were rushing here and there and Kate realized that she was usually the one out there rushing around. Grateful for this respite, she turned her attention to Edward, determined to enjoy every second she had with him.

"What were you thinking just now?" Edward asked as he brushed her hand with his fingers.

"Oh just that I felt grateful to be in here with you and out of the rat race for awhile."

"Truly?"

Smiling, Kate nodded. "I feel very fortunate to have run into you again last night. Fate and I are becoming friends again. You're fascinating and I'm excited to get to know you better."

Fingers tightening on Kate's hand, Edward smiled. "Thank you."

Kate squeezed Edward's hand and looked up at the approaching waiter.

"Good evening. Would you be interested in trying our house Pinot Noir?"

Edward looked at Kate and raised his eyebrows in question. Kate shrugged. She really didn't care, she was just happy to be here.

"You know, I don't think so. Tonight is a champagne night, wouldn't you agree, Kate?"

Nodding, Kate agreed. "Absolutely!"

"Right away, sir."

"Give him another five years, and he'll be a snooty maître'd somewhere," Kate giggled.

Edward laughed and Kate enjoyed hearing the sound. Edward had a great laugh, deep and full of life. Exactly how she imagined he was.

"Fantastic, Kate, very intuitive. How was your day?"

"It was great. We got quite a bit done for the launch of our new clothing line and then I splurged and pampered myself this afternoon."

"Really? How so?"

"Facial, massage, manicure and pedicure. The usual female stuff. It's been so long, I'd almost forgotten how lovely it feels."

"All women should be pampered routinely," Edward said.

"I can't believe you really feel that way," Kate said incredulously.

"I have a mother and two sisters, I've been brainwashed," Edward said wryly. "But beyond their brainwashing, I really do feel that way. Women should be cherished and pampered."

"You must be the only man on the planet who feels that way. Most are annoyed by the cost associated with routine pampering," Kate laughed.

The waiter returned with their champagne. Kate giggled to herself as she watched the waiter pop the cork and pour their drinks. He was definitely on the road to snootyville.

Edward raised his glass. "To Fate!"

"To Fate," Kate repeated.

As they touched glasses, Kate was blinded by a flash of light outside their window. Startled, she dropped her glass on the table. Thankfully it didn't break, but the champagne spilled everywhere.

Blinking furiously to clear her vision, Kate apologized. "Oh, I'm so sorry," she said as she whipped her napkin off her lap and tried to sop up the mess on the table.

"No worries, relax." Edward raised his hand and motioned the waiter over. The waiter came equipped with a new tablecloth, dishes, silverware and in no time their table was clean, dry and good as new.

Glancing outside, Kate saw a tall, dark man standing in front of the photographer. The man looked as if he was in the business of body-building. He was dressed in black cargo pants, a black t-shirt that stretched over his bulging muscles. Kate watched as the man escorted the photographer away from the window.

"What was that light?" Kate asked.

"A tourist, I think. Probably taking pictures of the restaurant. Our bad luck for sitting here. Are you okay?"

"Yes, I'm fine. Just a bit embarrassed," Kate said sheepishly.

"Nothing to be embarrassed about, it wasn't your fault." Edward refilled Kate's glass. "Shall we try again?"

"Please!" This time, their toast was successful.

"Have you been here before?" Edward asked.

"No, I've wanted to, but I never took the time," Kate answered. "Have you?"

"Oh, many times. It's another favorite of mine. I think you'll really enjoy the food here."

The waiter returned for their orders. Edward glanced at Kate, as if asking her permission to order for her. She agreed and Edward placed their orders.

"You're not making me eat liver or something equally disgusting, are you?" Kate asked after the waiter had walked away.

"Heavens no. Who can stand the stuff?" Edward laughed.

Kate took a sip of her champagne. "This is very delicious." She set her glass down and leaned back in her chair. "So, how was your day?"

"It was good. Not nearly as productive as yours, though," Edward laughed.

"Not much in the way of a facial man, are you?"

"No, that I'm not. I visited with some friends and hung

around the house. I cherish the days when I don't have to be
somewhere or doing something."

"Those are some of my favorite times as well. My daughter
and I love to lounge around the house and just be with each
other."

"You've a daughter? What's her name?"

"Her name is Mary. My miracle baby. She's five, beautiful
and full of life," Kate said. "My sister and her husband are
watching her while I'm here this week. They'll be heading out
on a two-week anniversary trip to Hawaii when I get back."

"Hawaii, a beautiful, exotic place. Hawaii is the only place
I've ever been to where just knowing I'm going there induces
instant relaxation. Do you have a photo of your daughter?"

"Only a million of them!" Kate laughed as she turned on
her phone and brought up the pictures of Mary.

The first picture that popped up was the one of her, Brad
and Mary at the hospital. She tried to swipe past it quickly,
but Edward stopped her. "Who is that?" Edward asked.

"My husband, Brad," Kate said sadly. "He died five years
ago."

Edward squeezed her hand. "I'm so sorry, Kate."

Shaking off her sadness, Kate offered a small smile.
"Thank you. He was a good man and it makes me sad to know
that Mary won't ever know him." Kate swiped past the picture
and showed off the rest that she'd saved on her phone.

"Brilliant photos. She's a beautiful child and from all I've
seen, a happy one."

"Indeed, she's the light of my life!" Kate took a sip of her
champagne. "Do you have any children?"

"No. I've haven't met the right woman, yet. But I hope one
day I'll be lucky enough," Edward said wistfully.

Smiling, Kate squeezed his hand. "I'm astounded some
woman hasn't snatched you up already," she laughed.

"That's what my mother says. I tell her that I'm picky and
that my heart will know when I've met the right one. My aunt
tells me I'm a hopeless romantic," Edward laughed.

They paused in their conversation while their food was
delivered. The aroma of the food was enticing and Kate
couldn't wait to taste the cuisine. The waiter refilled their
glasses, and then left them to their dinners.

Kate smiled and asked, "What am I eating, Edward?"

"Tonight, the lady is feasting on dressed Devon crab with
Amalfi lemon and melba toast. Next is aged Scottish rib-eye
with roasted chicory and caramelized red onion."

"Sounds delicious, thank you!"

"My pleasure, Kate."

They ate in silence for a while. As she was enjoying every bite, Kate tried to remember the last time she had felt so content and happy. Her uncharacteristic moment that night when she'd asked Edward to stay with her at her table was looking more and more like a really great decision. He was nice, complimentary and full of fascinating stories. He seemed genuinely pleased to be in her company. Her circle of friends was impossibly small, and she hoped that he would enter that small circle and remain there. Kate wouldn't wish for love, she felt that was reaching too far. But friendship...one could never have too much of that.

"Edward, this food is just delectable," Kate said as she finished her last bite and sat back in her chair.

"I'm glad you liked it," Edward said. "How about some flour-less chocolate cake with raspberries and mascarpone cream for dessert?"

"There's no way," Kate said laughing. "You'll have to roll me out of here if I eat that. How embarrassing would that be?"

"Not embarrassing in the least. Food is meant to be enjoyed. Besides, we could always take a stroll through the park after, to work off some of this food," Edward suggested.

Kate sat up and looked at Edward. His manner was so refreshing. She looked into his eyes and could see nothing but openness, honesty, and amusement. He really seemed to like her and she was enjoying his company immensely.

"What are you thinking, Kate?"

She hesitated, but was unsure why she did. She would like his friendship, but was afraid he'd read more into it than she meant him to. He seemed like such a good man, and Kate would hate for him to get the wrong impression. She was not in the business of hurting people. She'd been hurt too much in her life for her to gain any pleasure from someone's pain.

"I'm thinking that I really enjoy your company," Kate finally said.

Edward smiled. "More than that thought just flashed across your face. Please, share your thoughts with me."

The waiter appeared and saved Kate from answering right away. Edward glanced at Kate as the waiter cleared their plates. Raising his eyebrow, he silently asked her about dessert. She nodded her head, and Edward ordered, remembering her preference for tea with dessert. Kate sighed, and wondered at the thrill that coursed through her that he'd remembered.

Dropping her hands to her lap, she fiddled with her napkin. Not ready to meet his eyes, Kate looked out the window. "You're right, that wasn't all I was thinking. I guess I didn't think you'd be so perceptive, as we've only been friends a short time," Kate smiled weakly and continued. "My circle of friends is small, and I was thinking that I would really like for you to be a part of it. But at the same time, I'm not sure that I'm ready for more than that and I would hate to lead you to think I was or that I wanted more," Kate paused and took a breath, shaking her head. "And that was incredibly arrogant of me to assume that you are interested in more. I live in a different country and am only here four times a year." Embarrassed, Kate hung her head, feeling the heat creep up her face.

"Kate, look at me," Edward implored.

As she lifted her eyes, they met Edward's. His were such beautiful eyes and in them she saw friendship, understanding and something else she couldn't quite put her finger on. Whatever it was, it made her feel special and important.

"You're not arrogant, Kate, and I don't think you're out of line in the least to lay out your boundaries. I can tell that you've been through hell and back, and I hope that when you're ready, you'll confide in me. I would be honored to be your friend, to be included in your circle. I find you to be special, amusing, interesting, and don't be mad – but I find you incredibly sexy," Edward smiled. "This, right here," Edward gestured to the two of them and their finished dinner. "This is enough for me, right now. My circle is quite small as well."

Releasing a breath, Kate blinked her eyes. She placed her hand in his and squeezed. He was such a breath of fresh air and she was going to breathe in as much of him as she could before she headed back to the U.S. "Thank you, Edward."

They walked through Hyde Park and Kate couldn't believe it. If she were a superstitious person, she thought she'd be able to feel the ghosts of all the members of the *ton* who'd come before her. What it must have been like to have lived during that time.

She and Edward talked as they strolled. She told him about Mary and her life in the States. She told him about her work and her sister. He told more of his travels and some fun stories of when he was a boy.

Edward walked her back to her hotel. "I've thoroughly

enjoyed our evening."

"Me too. Thank you very much, Edward."

"Are you available tomorrow night?"

"I could be," Kate said jokingly.

"Let me take you out again. Would you like to catch a show?"

Smiling, Kate nodded her head. "Very much."

"Is five-thirty ok? We'll have dinner before the show."

"Perfect, I'll see you tomorrow."

Edward leaned down and brushed a soft kiss across her cheek. "Until tomorrow," he whispered.

Kate froze and as she watched him walk away, her hand came up to touch her cheek. She couldn't believe it, he'd kissed her. And he wanted to take her out again. It would be the third night in a row that they'd spent time together. She was getting spoiled.

Kate sighed as he disappeared into the crowd. As she turned to cross the lobby to the elevator, she thought she saw the same body-builder man following behind Edward that she saw from the restaurant. She rose up on tippy-toes to get a better look, but they turned a corner and were out of sight. Shrugging her shoulders, she put it out of her mind and got on the elevator. Her life would be so boring when she got home, she mused. She'd be busy enough with Mary, work and her friends and family. But she was enjoying this time here, enjoying meeting a man she liked. Enjoying being romanced.

It made her sad to think they'd lose touch, again, when she left on Saturday. She honestly couldn't imagine he'd keep in touch for long, if at all. But oh, imagine the possibilities if he did.

Chapter Fourteen

Kate woke on Saturday morning torn between happiness at seeing Mary in a few hours and slightly depressed at not spending more time with Edward.

Their date the night before had been beyond compare. They had enjoyed a quiet dinner at Auberge in Waterloo before the play. They started with French baguettes and calamari. Kate had worked through lunch, completely forgetting to eat, and had been half starved when they arrived at the restaurant. Then they had moved on to their main courses. Kate chose the filet de saumon, a Scottish salmon fillet with a white wine, cream and dill sauce. It was served with chive buttered new potatoes and steamed spinach. Edward had the Poisson parmentier, a fish pie of cod, haddock, prawn and salmon in a creamy sauce of white wine and leek, topped with mashed potato and cheese.

Kate couldn't believe the taste of the food lately. In the five years she'd been traveling to London, she'd never had food as good as she'd had all the nights she'd dined with Edward. She wasn't sure if the company was what improved the food, or if she had been cheaping out. Either way, Kate was sure she was going home with a couple extra pounds. Usually she and Edward would share a dessert, but last night, they couldn't agree on just one. Kate ended up ordering the crème brûlée, and Edward ordered the mousse au chocolat. In the end, they did share, and Kate was glad. His chocolate mousse was as delicious as her crème brûlée.

"I am glad we walked," Kate said to Edward once they'd finally finished their desserts.

"Why?"

"Because I need to walk off some of this food!" Kate sighed as she sipped her tea. "I'm having a delicious time, thank you!"

Laughing, Edward rose from his chair. "That makes two of us. Come on, let's get moving. We don't want to miss the show!"

They walked briskly to the theatre. The Old Vic was showing *Kiss Me, Kate*, which Edward thought was fitting. He'd given her a few pecks here and there, but there was nothing he wanted more than to sink into her lips. Edward reached for her hand as they strolled down the street.

He glanced across the street and saw a photographer snapping their picture and watched as his bodyguard, Jason, moved the photographer along, discouraging anymore photographs from being taken. Edward sighed but thanked his lucky stars that Kate was headed out tomorrow and would most likely miss this set of pictures being published. Sometimes he wished he'd become the lawyer his mother wanted him to be. His life would be his own, and strolling down the street wouldn't give him an anxiety attack.

Edward knew he should be up front with Kate about his career. It was definitely some information she needed, especially where Mary was concerned. He wasn't overly famous in America yet, but it was coming fast. And once it did, neither Kate nor Mary would be safe from the paparazzi. This was something that Kate would have to consider in being associated with him.

He wanted normal for as long as he could get it. And he liked the anonymity of Kate not knowing who he really was. He could tell she liked him for who he was. She didn't put on airs, didn't expect him to lavish gifts on her, didn't expect the best tables and restaurants to cater to her. She was such a breath of fresh air. He loved that she expected nothing from him but good company.

It was something that was lacking in his life. He loved his mother and his sisters, but even they had come to expect the best. They weren't selfish or demanding about it. Money changed people, and there were times he wished he could go back to before.

Edward held the door for Kate and they stepped inside the theatre. He watched Kate as she openly gawked at the lobby. Thankfully, she was so busy taking in her surroundings, she didn't notice all the people stop and stare at him. Fixing a 'don't come near me stare' on his face, he guided Kate to their box. Settling her in, he took a seat next to her. "Have you seen this play before?"

"No, and honestly, it's my first play," Kate admitted.

"Are you serious?"

Kate nodded. "Well, I've seen the productions the kids did when I was in high school, but I've never seen a professional one."

"I'm astounded," Edward said. From the little he'd gleaned from her over the past few nights, Kate didn't do or go many places. He wondered if that was by choice, or if she never had the opportunity. "I'll be doubly interested in whether you like this or not, then." Edward said.

"Oh, I'm sure I will. Like traveling, this is something I've always wanted to do. It's hard to get away. But then again, I work so much that I really only want to spend my free time with Mary," Kate explained.

"I understand. What else is on your bucket list?"

Kate laughed. "Oh so much, you can't even imagine!"

The lights dimmed and Edward watched as people rushed to their seats. He glanced at Kate and was amused to see she was still taking it all in. He settled back into his seat and decided the show he really wanted to watch was Kate. He could imagine what was on her list. He'd once had a long list of things he wanted to do and see. And he'd steadily crossed them off. He wanted to help Kate cross items off her list. He wondered if falling in love and getting married again was on her list.

Trying to reign in his thoughts, he leaned forward and asked her if she'd like a glass of wine or some water. She chose water, so he excused himself and went in search of some refreshments. He'd learned that the best time to get drinks was after the lights dimmed, just before the show started. Most everyone was in their seats and he wasn't usually bothered by people asking for autographs and such.

Securing their drinks, he headed back to their box. He dreaded the fact she was leaving tomorrow. He'd enjoyed their evenings together and wanted to spend more time with her. She had told him she came to town about every twelve weeks. He wasn't sure he could wait that long to see her again. Maybe they could exchange some phone calls between now and then. That would take some of the edge off. She seemed to be a little reserved, so he didn't think that a trip to America would be happening anytime soon.

As he entered the box, Kate glanced at him with a smile on her face. "I'm so glad you made it back. It looks like it's going to start any second!"

Edward passed Kate her water. "The lines aren't long if you wait until the lights dim," Edward told her.

"Oh, you've been to a few of these shows, huh? You know all the secrets!" Kate laughed.

"Indeed, I do," Edward said. He wondered how she'd react if he just leaned over and crushed her lips beneath his. The temptation to do so was so strong, it took his breath away.

"Ooh, look, Edward! I think it's starting!"

Sipping his drink, Edward sat back in his seat and concentrated on the show that was Kate Walker. He was sure he was in for a very interesting show.

Kate could feel Edward's stare while she tried to pay attention to the beginning of the show. He was so attentive and it was something she didn't want to take for granted. She'd had love once and as time went by she realized that she'd taken it all for granted. That he would be there for her, to help her raise Mary, to share the highs and the lows with, to grow old with. She taken it all for granted. It was something that she'd promised herself she'd try to never let happen again.

She never wanted to take anything for granted. Not Mary, Erin, Georgie, her job, her travels, or even Edward. She tried to always be in the moment and to cherish every memory, no matter how small and insignificant. If Kate had learned anything from Brad's death, it was that those small insignificant memories were what kept you going when you didn't think you could take another step.

She'd only known Edward a short time, and she knew herself well enough to know that she wasn't quite ready to take the plunge into a relationship, especially not a long distance one. But if she was going to choose anyone, it would be him. She couldn't help but wonder if they'd stay in touch over the next twelve weeks or so until she came back to London. She wondered if he really was fine with just being friends with her. Maybe all he wanted was someone to have dinner with, go sight-seeing with, someone to hang with every few months. And she wondered how she'd feel if that was truly all he wanted. The thought depressed her a bit, and she was surprised by that.

Just then, Edward shifted in his chair. She felt him lean closer and whisper into her ear.

"What's wrong, Kate?"

Kate turned her head slightly. "Nothing, why?

"You seem sad. Are you not enjoying the show?"

"No, I'm fine," Kate whispered. *Liar!* Her mind shouted at her. "And I'm enjoying the show very much!" *Double Liar, you haven't even been paying attention!*

"Look at me," Edward demanded.

Kate turned to look him straight in the eye.

"You're not watching the show, Kate."

Kate rolled her eyes. "How do you know that?"

"Because I've been watching you the whole time. You're staring into space, lost in your thoughts. And something you just thought made you unhappy," Edward whispered urgently. "What's wrong?"

"I was just thinking that tonight is our last evening together."

"Does that make you sad, Kate?"

"Yes."

Edward leaned closer and gently touched his lips to hers. She was surprised, but didn't pull away. She had wondered what it would be like to kiss Edward, and he was surpassing her expectations. His lips were warm and firm. He didn't pressure her with an aggressive kiss. He gently coaxed a response from her. She kissed him back and sighed softly against his lips.

He pulled back slightly and whispered against her lips. "Me too, Kate. I would like more time with you."

Taking her lips again, more firmly this time, she felt Edward trying to convey his feelings with his lips. Kate knew just how he felt. She returned the kiss with equal fervor, wrapping her arms around his neck. She let her fingers play with the hair at the nape of his neck and turned her head slightly to the side for better access.

God! She'd missed this. The connection between two people. The attraction. The passion. She could feel herself sinking into him, falling into the sensations. If they didn't stop soon, the theater-goers were going to get more of a show than they bargained for. A part of her didn't care, though.

Five years is a long time to go without this connection. And she was a person who needed, craved this connection. Why had she kept herself closed off for so long?

Edward gently raised his head. "If we don't stop now, we'll be in trouble," he whispered.

Still a bit dazed at her reaction to him and his kisses, she nodded.

He pulled his chair up next to hers and wrapped his arm around her shoulders. He gently tugged her closer to him until she was leaning against him with her head cradled beneath his chin.

They stayed that way through the rest of the show. When it was over, Kate was reluctant to leave his side. What was happening to her? Was she so lonely and deprived that she was going to cling to him? Maybe some time apart would be a good thing.

It seemed Edward was in no rush either. He kept his arm around her and she silently watched as the people filed out of the theater. She wondered if he'd fallen asleep. She peeked up at his face and was startled to find his eyes on hers.

"Ready to go?" she asked quietly.

"Not even a little bit," he said.

"No, me neither," Kate said and laid her head back on his chest. "But my flight leaves pretty early and I can't miss it," Kate said.

"I know," he sighed. He kissed the top of her head. "Alright, let's get you back to your hotel. I don't want to be responsible for your little girl's tears because her mum missed her plane."

Edward took hold of her hand and held it the whole way to the hotel. Kate grinned inwardly, secretly happy that he was as attached to her as she was to him. She felt the same level of attachment.

"Edward?" Kate said as she chanced a quick peek at his face. They were only a couple blocks from the the hotel.

He returned her look. "Hmm?"

"I think that twelve weeks is a long time. I wonder how you'd feel if maybe we had a few phone calls between now and when I come back?"

She watched as a smile lit up Edward's face and Kate knew she'd been right to suggest it.

"Splendid idea! I was just trying to figure out how I was could suggest the same thing. I didn't want to scare you off," Edward said.

"Truly?" Kate asked. This whole thing seemed too good to be true and she was a little afraid to trust it.

He stopped and raised their clasped hands to his lips. Lightly brushing a kiss across the back of her hand, he nodded. "Truly, Kate. I would love to be able to talk on the phone with you over the next few weeks. Actually, I'd love to be able to spend time with you, but this is the next best thing. I'll take it."

A huge smile broke out on Kate's face and she heard Edward suck in a breath. "You are so beautiful," he said just before he lowered his head and kissed her senseless again.

Kate lost all sense of time and space. She felt dizzy when Edward lifted his head and gazed into her eyes. "We'd better get going," he said softly.

Again unable to form coherent words, Kate nodded. Edward grinned at her reaction and led her away toward the hotel.

By the time they reached the hotel, Kate had herself pulled together. She felt a tiny bit foolish at her reaction to him, but at the same time she reveled in the feelings. Twelve weeks felt like a long time.

Chapter Fifteen

"Mary, it's time for dinner. Come, let's wash your hands."

"Mo-om!" Mary whined. "I want to play!"

Kate laughed. "We can play after we eat," Kate said as she guided Mary over to the sink.

It had been a month since she returned from England. She hadn't spoken to Edward since their last "date" the night before she left. She hadn't really expected they'd talk all the time, but was still a bit surprised that they hadn't spoken yet. She was busy with Mary and she'd gotten a promotion at work. She was now in charge of all the marketing for the new clothing line. The days flew by too quickly.

Mary's birthday was coming up and Kate hadn't planned anything yet. She made a mental note to pick up some invitations this weekend and get it planned. The phone rang as she was helping Mary into the booster seat at the table. Kate let it go to voicemail. Because Kate worked long hours during the day, she made sure dinner was a special time and Kate avoided distractions as much as she could. They typically rushed out of the house in the mornings, and Kate would try to have lunch with Mary at least twice a week. Kate made sure to spend as much down time with Mary as she could.

It wasn't until Kate was getting herself ready for bed that

she remembered the phone call. Curious, she picked up her cell. Her heart in her throat, she listened to the message. "Kate? Hello, this is Edward calling. I apologize it's taken me so long to get in touch with you. I was called out of town Monday after you left and I just got back last night. I hope you and Mary are doing well. I'll be in and out all day tomorrow, but would be honored if you'd give me a ring back. Take care."

She couldn't believe it. He'd called. She felt like a giddy school girl with her first crush. Glancing at the clock, she quickly did the math. Ugh, four in the morning. She would have to wait until morning to call. Sliding between the sheets, she set her alarm and then drifted off to sleep.

Kate's morning dragged by. She had decided to call Edward on her lunch break and when it finally arrived, Kate grabbed her lunch out of the fridge and rushed up to the rooftop garden to make her call.

She dialed the number and waited out the rings. Disappointment coursed through her when his voicemail picked up. "Hello, this is Edward. I'm unavailable to take your call right now. Please leave a message and I'll get back to you as soon as I'm able."

"Um, hello Edward? This is Kate, returning your call. I'm on my lunch break, so if you get this message in the next little bit feel free to call me back. Mary is usually in bed by eight my time, and I'm free after that. Looking forward to talking to you. Bye."

Hanging up, she set the phone down next to her. She took a bite out of her salad and relaxed at the table. She glanced around the garden, taking in the view. The roses were blooming, the air was clear and she could see across the city with ease. It was a beautiful day. She enjoyed the peace that came with taking her lunch on the rooftop garden. No ringing phones, no one poking their heads in her office, no deadlines. It was just Kate and nature. She relished the feel of the warm sun shining on her. Taking Mary to the beach this weekend would be a fun excursion, she thought to herself.

Kate was packing up her leftovers when her phone rang. She quickly snatched it up. "Hello?" she answered breathlessly.

"Kate? It's Edward."

"Edward! Hello! How are you doing?"

"I'm good. And you?"

"Same. Enjoying some sunshine before I head back in to work."

"I'm sorry it's taken me so long to get in touch with you. I've been away."

"I'm glad you called. Where did you go?"

"I was in Jamaica. Beautiful country and amazing people. I almost didn't want to come home. Of course, it's raining and chilly here, so now I do wish I was back in Jamaica," Edward laughed.

Kate laughed with him. "It sunny and seventy here today. It's perfect weather. I'm thinking of taking Mary to the beach this weekend. She loves to play in the sand."

"That sounds like a fun idea. How have you been, Kate?"

"I've been good, busy. With Mary, with work. I got a promotion, I'm now in charge of marketing for our new clothing line."

"That's brilliant, Kate! Congratulations!"

"Thank you. And you, how have you been?"

"I'm glad to be home. I love to travel, but it's always nice to be home. Stopped in at Tempo last night. Ricardo, the server, asked about you. I told him you'd gone home to America, but would hopefully be back soon," Edward said wistfully.

"It won't be for another six to eight weeks."

"Six to eight weeks? That's too long, and I think I'll be out of town when you're here next. When will you know the exact dates?"

"I imagine Erin will be telling me within the week so I can make the arrangements," Kate said as she twisted a lock of hair around her finger. "Are you really that anxious to see me, Edward?"

"I am. It's crazy, I know. You've really made an impression on me, Kate. The whole time I was in Jamaica, I thought of you constantly. You would pop into my head at the craziest moments and my concentration would be blown."

"The same thing happens to me with you. I'm sure the time will go by quickly, Edward," Kate said trying to be positive.

"Impossible. It's already felt like forever since I saw you last. Would you think it completely daft of me if I were to travel to you before I leave again?"

Kate was speechless. Was he really that eager to spend time with her? She couldn't form a coherent thought. Had they really clicked so completely? She had told the truth when she said it had been the same for her. He popped into her thoughts at odd moments throughout the day and evening. Not hearing from him since she'd returned had made her think she'd made up the whole thing. If not for Erin asking her on and off if she'd heard from him, she really would have thought she'd made it all up.

"Kate? Are you there? I scared you, didn't I? Ugh, I'm so daft. I knew it. I told myself not to say anything. I'm sorry, Kate."

"No, no. Edward, stop please. I'm fine, it's fine. I was trying to find the words, I'd love for you to come visit me. I'm still having a hard time believing that you're real," Kate laughed.

"Ah, Kate," Edward sighed.

"You'll really come to visit?" Kate asked.

"I'm on the next plane," Edward promised.

About an hour after she returned from lunch, Kate received an email from Edward with his flight details.

Kate,
Leaving for the airport now. My flight gets in around 10:30p your time. I'll catch a cab to your apartment. See you soon!
-Edward

Shivers of excitement ran through her. How could this be possible? How could she be so lucky twice in her life? Kate couldn't get rid of her smile for the rest of the day. Erin sent several questioning looks her way, but couldn't ask since she was on conference calls all afternoon. Kate was grateful for those calls, she wanted to savor this moment.

Erin finally caught up with her as Kate was heading toward the elevators to go home. "Soooo, what's with all the smiling this afternoon?"

Kate laughed. "I had a phone call at lunch that just made my day."

"Oh? Would it be the mysterious Edward?"

"It would," Kate said. Barely able to contain her excitement, she whirled around and faced Erin. Grabbing Erin's arm, she excitedly told her about the phone call. "And he's on a plane, right now!" Shaking her head, she pierced Erin with her gaze. "Can you believe this? Because, I can't. I'm excited to see him again. Like crazy excited. But at the same time, I'm scared. Is that crazy? Am I crazy?"

"No, Kate. You're not crazy. And you should be excited. You met a man. A man who seems normal and likable, and who obviously adores you."

"You don't think it's weird, though? I mean, we met by

chance. We've had four dates over a period of four months. I don't really know him. And now, he's flying across the ocean to visit with me for the weekend. I'm going to introduce him to my daughter," Kate said.

"Kate," Erin grinned. "You need to calm down. Just go with it. He could be your Happy Ever After. Don't mess it up with all your questions and panic. Enjoy it. You've been sad a long time...you deserve some happy."

Kate paused and searched Erin's face. Realizing she only saw truth in her eyes, Kate nodded. "I'm over-thinking it, you're right. We hit it off and I really like him." Kate blew out a deep breath. "Okay, I'm okay now. Thank you, Erin."

"You're welcome," Kate laughed. "So, I guess you won't be in tomorrow?"

"What? No, I'll be here. I'm sure he'll be exhausted and want to sleep."

Erin stared at Kate for a moment. Shaking her head, she said "Kate, now you really are crazy. The man is flying seven hours to see you. The last thing he's gonna want to do is sleep. Take tomorrow and have a great weekend. I want all the deets on Monday!" Erin opened the door to the daycare and waved to her daughters. She signed her name to the list, showed her driver's license and then lifted her daughters over the gate.

Kate copied the same process Erin did and when she picked up Mary, her heart almost burst from the happiness. An unexpected three-day weekend that she would spend with Mary and an incredibly fascinating man.

Could life be any better?

Chapter Sixteen

Kate sailed through the evening on cloud nine. She couldn't wait to see Edward, to introduce him to Mary. The closer it got to Edward's arrival, the less Kate could sit still. She'd worn an imaginary path in the carpet between the couch and the window. Even though she was expecting him, she was still startled at the knock on the door. Her palms grew sweaty and she couldn't catch her breath as she raced toward the door. Fumbling with the lock in her haste, she finally managed to wrench the door open.

And there he stood. Complete perfection and exactly as she remembered him. "Edward!"

He stepped forward with a bouquet of flowers. Kate barely saw them as she was enveloped in his arms. "I've missed you," he whispered into her hair.

Kate sighed and sank into his hug. It felt so good to be held and missed. "Come inside, you must be exhausted," Kate said as she ushered him and his belongings into her apartment. "Here, come sit on the couch. Do you want some wine?"

"Please!" Instead of sitting down, he walked over to the windows and looked out. "Nice view, Kate."

"Thanks!" Kate called out as she walked into the kitchen for the wine bottle and another glass. "I love living in the city and being close to everything. I'm only a few blocks from work, Mary and I usually walk everyday."

She passed him his glass of wine.

"Come sit with me, Kate," Edward said as he sat down on the couch.

More than happy to oblige him, she snuggled under his arm, resting her head on his chest. "I'm so happy you came," Kate whispered. She was surprised at how comfortable and safe she felt sitting here with Edward. "Erin gave me the day off tomorrow, I'm completely free to do whatever you'd like. We can play at being tourists, or see a show, or just be lazy. Whatever you want to do is fine."

"I just want to spend time with you. You mentioned going to the beach with Mary. We should do that," Edward suggested.

"Absolutely. At some point this weekend, I need to pick up some invitations and get them out for Mary's birthday party. It shouldn't take me long," Kate laughed. "I have no idea what I'm going to do for her birthday. She's still young, so probably just a small, intimate party here again this year, with her friends from daycare and our family."

Edward took a sip of his wine, and studied Kate's face. How amazing that he'd gotten attached to her so quickly. He didn't regret packing up and flying to see her. Not for a second. He did regret waiting a month to talk to her. He hadn't been able to get her out of his mind after their final date in London. He'd gone home and dreamt of her, as he'd done almost every night since.

She was so refreshing. Open, honest. It'd been a long time since he'd met anyone like her. Most of the people in his circle only told him what they thought he wanted to hear. It was obvious to him that Kate still had no idea who he was. And that made her even more attractive to him.

"Georgie, my sister, said she'd take Mary tomorrow or Saturday night if we wanted to go out and have a nice dinner," Kate said as she leaned back to look into his face.

"Do you want to do that, Kate? I'm happy to be here with you two girls."

"Weekends are usually our bonding time, Mary and me. But this weekend is special, so I think I will let Georgie have her. All three of us can hang out tomorrow and Saturday morning. Then I'll let Georgie take Mary, and we can enjoy your last night here before you head back to London."

"As long as it makes you happy, I'm open to whatever you

decide. Don't feel like you have to make any special considerations for me," Edward said. "Can I ask you a personal question?"

"Of course," Kate replied.

"Why don't Georgie and Tim have children of their own?"

Kate sighed. "They can't. They tried for years. They saw doctors, specialists, medicine doctors. They tried IVF. Prayers, cleansings, fastings. Everything. Nothing worked. They stopped trying right before I got pregnant with Mary."

"They never wanted to adopt?"

"Georgie did, but by the time they stopped trying, Tim was over it," Kate shook her head. "That was mean. He was just worn out and burned out. He told Georgie that this was how God wanted their life, and that after everything they'd tried and done, it just wasn't meant to be."

"That's so sad," Edward said.

"It is. I know Georgie is extremely close to Mary because of it. And honestly, I can't blame her."

Edward nodded, and rubbed his hand along her arm.

Kate smiled and rested her head back on his chest. "It's so surreal," Kate murmured.

"What is?"

"You being here. I feel so happy and content to have you here, but there's another part of me that is a tiny bit scared and worried." She felt Edward tense under her cheek and quickly continued. "Not because I'm afraid of you or I'm worried you're some axe murderer," Kate laughed. "I...it's just fast. And that scares me a little bit. It scares me how happy I am to have you here, how much I care about you already, how much I feel like I know you," Kate finished.

"I understand. It was rather rash of me to fly here. I've thought about you constantly since you left. I had to see if it was real, what I remembered, or if I'd somehow made it more than it was. Talking to you on the phone, I knew I hadn't exaggerated anything in my mind. Seeing you framed in the door, I knew I'd made the right choice to come."

The weekend was flying by too quickly. All too soon, Georgie was at the door to pick up Mary for the night. They'd enjoyed a lazy breakfast before heading to the beach. Mary had instantly wrapped Edward around her finger, and had used it quite to her advantage. Kate was a little afraid of how easily that particular skill had come to her. It didn't bode well for her teenage years, for sure.

"Edward, I'd like for you to meet my sister. This is Georgie," Kate laughed at Georgie's eye roll.

"Edward, so nice to meet you," Georgie said as she shook Edward's hand. "Are you enjoying your visit?"

"Very much," Edward said.

"Ah G!!! Ah G!!!" Mary yelled as she ran and launched herself at Georgie. "I'm sleeping at your house!"

"Hi Sweet Pea! A little excited?"

"Yes," Mary said. "Mom's having a date!"

Georgie laughed. "Well, I'm glad you're excited. Uncle Tim is taking us out to dinner tonight," Georgie said as she lifted Mary's bag and slung it over her shoulder.

"PIZZA!" Mary yelled.

"Pizza, it's the only one way to this girl's heart!"

Edward sent a playful glare at Kate. "Why didn't you tell me that? We could have had pizza for breakfast yesterday!"

Laughing, Kate said "You didn't need any help. She had you wrapped around her finger in five seconds. I'm still a little appalled at how quickly that all transpired. Makes me weep for the teenage boys." Kate motioned toward Mary's overnight bag. "All her gear is in there, lovey, clothes and some snacks. Want me to come down with you?"

"No, no. We're good," Georgie said as she opened the door. "So nice to meet you Edward, enjoy the rest of your visit."

"Thank you, Georgie. It was a pleasure to meet you as well," Edward held the door open for the duo.

"I'll text you tomorrow and let you know when I'll be by to pick her up," Kate said as she gave Mary one last hug and kiss.

"No rush. We don't get nearly enough time with her," Georgie said. "See you tomorrow!"

"Bye Mama! Wuv you!"

"Bye Mary, have fun. I love you too!" She watched as they cruised down the hall to the elevator and waved goodbye as they stepped into the elevator. Sighing, she shut the door.

"You didn't have to send her away, Kate," Edward soothed as he wrapped his arms around her.

"I know," Kate sighed. "I want to spend some time with you, just us. And Georgie is always asking for her share of time with Mary. I'm stingy, she's my baby and I want her all to myself. I go a little nuts when she's not here. It's so much easier when I go away. I have work to focus on, touristy things to do. But to be in this apartment when she's not, it feels wrong."

"Empty nest syndrome. That's what my mum calls it. She said she had it bad after everyone left the house. She told me that she'd spent so many years, so much time and energy on us that when we'd all finally gone – she didn't know what to do with herself. Had no idea how to occupy her time."

"Ugh, you mean it'll get worse with time?"

"Undoubtedly."

"I can't even imagine it," Kate shook her head. She took a deep breath and let it out slowly. "I just need something to do. Something to take my mind off her not being here. Shall we go out?"

Edward leaned his head down and nuzzled her ear. Taking a couple quick nips of her earlobe, he whispered "No."

Kate shivered. It was delicious, the feelings that he was creating in her. He slowly backed her up to the wall. Running his hands down her sides, he continued to explore her face with his lips. Slowly he kissed his way across her cheek and when his lips reached hers, passion exploded between them.

Breaking away from the kiss, Edward groaned. "Kate, do you want me to stop?"

"No, don't stop. Please!" She tugged his shirt out of his jeans. Running her hands up his chest, she sighed in appreciation. His chest was like marble, finely chiseled. Warm and tan, she reveled in the feel of it as she ran her hands over his chest and back.

"Our first time isn't going to be up against a wall, Kate. Hang on to me," Edward said as he lifted her in his arms. He carried her to her bedroom and gently laid her on the bed. He slowly raised her shirt over her head and flung it across the room. Looking down at her, he sighed in appreciation. "God Kate, you're so beautiful." He traced his lips across her collar bones and then down between her breasts. Sighing softly, he rested his forehead on her stomach. "I've dreamt of this since the first night we shared dinner. Do you even know how alluring you are?"

Sighing with pleasure and not a little womanly pride, Kate raised her hand to his face and traced a line from his brow to his lips. "Kiss me, Edward."

Chapter Seventeen

Kate woke the next morning feeling happy and sated. She and Edward had spent the majority of the night becoming very intimately acquainted. Smiling to herself as she rolled over and snuggled closer to Edward, she thought back to the events of the night. Edward was so thoughtful and giving, their lovemaking had been amazing. She dropped a kiss to his shoulder and she slowly closed her eyes.

Edward draped his arm around her, tugging Kate closer. "Are you awake?" He asked sleepily, nuzzling the top of her head.

"Not really, I was just rolling over to get comfy."

"Do you want to be awake?" He asked as he slowly ran his hand up and down the curve of her back.

Smiling, Kate whispered, "That depends on what you're offering me. It's not often that I get to sleep in these days."

Edward gently pushed Kate onto her back. Leaning down to kiss her, he stopped just before their lips touched. "Oh, I don't think you'll mind missing some sleep-in time for what I have in mind," he said.

Kate sighed against his lips at his words, eagerly awaiting what Edward had in mind.

A couple of hours later, showered and dressed, they left her apartment in search of food. While they were waiting for the elevator, Edward took her hand in his.

"I called the airline while you were in the shower and changed my flight to six tomorrow morning."

"But what about your meeting?" Kate asked.

"No worries, I changed that too. I explained that I got caught up on a personal project, one that's quite special to my heart and wouldn't be able to tear myself away until tomorrow."

"You won't get in any trouble?"

"No," he winked at her as the doors to the elevator opened and they stepped out into the lobby. "They can't have the meeting without me."

Kate smiled and looked up at him. "Where would you like to eat?"

"Matters not to me, love."

"Hmm," Kate thought. "How about somewhere small, romantic and local?"

"Sounds perfect! Which way," Edward asked as he looked up and down the street.

Kate tugged his hand and nodded to the right. "This way."

They strolled down the sidewalk hand in hand enjoying the warm sun and fresh air.

"You know Edward, I was thinking. You made this special trip out here, and you won't be around when I'm in London next. Perhaps Mary and I could make a special trip out to see you when you get back?"

"Are you sure you want to use up your holiday time? You only get a couple of weeks, right?"

"Well, yes, but I think it's worth it. Mary and I haven't ever traveled anywhere. We go to the beach and to my sister's house. I have plenty of time saved up and I think it would be fun for the two of us to get away and come visit you."

"Kate, I would adore it if you both came to visit. As soon as I get back, I'll verify my schedule and give you some definite dates," Edward said.

"I already have Mary's passport done. I got it when I found out that the travel to London was mandatory, in case I had to bring her along at some point."

"Wonderful, so there's no waiting on a passport," Edward said as he squeezed her hand. "I'll take you both out to my country home. I have a couple of horses, we could take her riding."

"Oh, she'd love that," Kate laughed and dropped her head

onto his shoulder. "She rode a pony at the petting zoo and then she begged me for a pony of her own for weeks." Kate stopped walking and tugged on Edward's hand.

"What's wrong, Kate?" Edward asked as he looked down at her face.

"Edward, I don't want to sound crazy, but I think that man over there is taking pictures of us," Kate said as she nodded across the street.

Edward cringed inwardly. While he still wasn't well-known in America, there was always the chance someone would recognize him. He ducked his head and tried to reassure Kate. "Maybe he's a tourist?"

"Could be," Kate mused. "Although why he wants a picture of me is the question. I don't look like a local."

"No, but you are beautiful. I don't blame him for wanting to take a picture to remember you by."

Smiling, Kate looked into his eyes. "You're sweet, thank you!" She stood on her tiptoes and gave him a kiss on the lips. "There's more of that later," she promised.

"I can't wait," he whispered. He gently cupped the back of her neck and kissed her again, more urgently. "I can't get enough of you, love."

"I know, me either." Kate rested her forehead against his chest. "Come, let's eat. It's just down the block here."

Edward took her hand and they hurried down the sidewalk.

"Emilio's?" Edward inquired as he opened the door for Kate.

"It's one of my favorites around here. I found this place not long after Mary and I moved into our apartment."

"Italian?" Edward grinned. "Why didn't I guess?"

Kate laughed.

"Maybe we can go to Italy someday. We'll get you some real Italian food," Edward said.

"Oh, that would be lovely!"

"Kate, hello! Where's little Mary?"

"Hello, Nan!" Kate said as she kissed the woman's cheek. "Mary is staying the weekend with my sister. But I've brought you someone new to spoil!" Kate reached behind her and tugged Edward up next to her. "Nan, this is Edward, and Edward, this is Nan."

Edward shook hands with Nan. She was a very tiny woman, couldn't have been more than five feet tall. Very petite, she had snow white hair that hung thickly down her

back. Her eyes were a clear, bright blue and reminded Edward
of the sunny, cloudless skies back home.

"Nice to meet you, Nan," Edward said.

A twinkle and a knowing gleam entered Nan's eyes as she
gathered up the daily menu and led them to their table. "What
can I get you to drink, my dears?"

"I'd love some lemon water to start, Nan." Kate said.

"I'll have the same, please," Edward said.

"Our special today is the meat lasagna, gouda cheese
ravioli and chicken marsala. Our soup today is wedding soup.
I'll be right back with your drinks."

"Oh, I love their wedding soup," Kate said. "The meatballs
are perfectly bite-sized."

"You must come here often?"

"Oh yes, at least once a week. Mary and I adore this place.
Nan is like the mother mine wishes she could be. It's sad, but
true. Everyone here treats Mary like she's their favorite
granddaughter. Nan's husband, Mario, is the evening chef.
They've been trying to find a daytime chef, but no one
compares to Emilio, their son. He's abroad right now, training
under some big-shot chef in France. They are so proud of
him."

"This sounds like a wonderful place."

Kate nodded as she placed her napkin in her lap. "It is.
The first couple of times I went to London, Pappagallo's
reminded me of Emilio's. I guess that's part of the reason I
went there so often. I was homesick and missing Mary, and
that place felt like home."

Edward laced his fingers with hers. "Home is important,"
Edward said solemnly. "What's good here?" Edward asked as
he gestured to the menu.

"I've never had a bad meal here, and I've eaten just about
everything they offer. Mary's favorite is the ravioli. I'm partial
to the lasagna, and of course the wedding soup."

"And are you getting the lasagna today?"

"You better believe it," Kate said laughing. "I need the
extra carbs for the things I have planned for us tonight."

Spying Nan coming toward their table, his whispered
"You're wicked!" was the only reply he could give.

Putting their waters down on the table, Nan gathered up
their menus. "Ready to order?"

Kate nodded to Edward and he gave Nan their order. "I'd
like to try the ravioli. Kate would like the lasagna and we'd
like to share a bowl of the wedding soup, please."

"Excellent choices," Nan replied. "Would you like any wine with your meal?"

"Please, do you offer Pinot Noir?"

"We do. Would you like a glass or the bottle?"

Glancing at Kate, Edward smiled playfully. "Oh, I think the bottle will do us quite well, thank you."

Kate nudged Edward's leg with her foot as Nan walked away. "A whole bottle? It's good we're walking!"

Edward laughed, I doubt we'll get too smashed sharing a bottle between us and all this food we're about to eat."

"I suppose you're right. It just sounds so decadent."

"We're together and sharing a romantic meal. This is the best weekend of my life. We should indulge, Kate."

"You're too sweet," Kate said as she rubbed her hand on his forearm.

He laced his fingers with hers and raised his water glass. "To Fate."

Kate tapped her glass to his. "To Fate," she murmured.

The rest of the weekend was heaven. After the late lunch at Emilio's, they went to the art gallery. They spent the afternoon looking through the gallery and speaking to the owner. They stopped at the old theater and took in a showing of The King and I. It was well past dark when they arrived back at the apartment.

Kate went into the kitchen to call Georgie about keeping Mary an extra night. While she was doing that, Edward poured them more wine and stood at the window enjoying the view.

"How's Mary?" Edward asked when she joined him at the window. He handed her a glass of wine.

"Perfect. She loves them, and it makes me so happy and relieved to know that. Georgie is off work tomorrow, some federal holiday that only government workers and bankers get off. She's fine with keeping Mary again tonight and watching her tomorrow while I'm at work."

"You're sad though," Edward prompted.

"No, not sad. Just down, I guess," Kate shrugged. "I don't know exactly how I'm feeling. I know that I don't want tomorrow to come, but it will."

"I know," Edward ran his hand through Kate's hair. "I'm not ready for our weekend to end, either."

"This long distance stuff is hard."

"Indeed. We can do it though."

"I don't want you to go, Edward." Kate laid her head on his chest, breathing in his unique scent. "I'm not crazy, am I? I sometimes feel crazy. Like I'm some love-sick teenager who has no boundaries."

"If you're crazy, then I'm headed to the madhouse with you. I feel the same." He wrapped his arms around her and they sat in silence, each lost in their own thoughts.

A playful smile appeared on Edward's face. "I think I can take your mind off your woes, if you'll allow me."

Kate's smile mirrored Edward's. "I'll allow this."

Chapter Eighteen

"You don't look happy," Erin remarked upon seeing the look on Kate's face when she walked into the office.

"I am happy, just sad the weekend is over." Kate sat her bag down on her desk and looked up at Erin. "We had such an amazing time, Erin. Neither one of us was ready for it to be over."

Erin dropped down into one of Kate's guest chairs and glared up at Kate. "I canceled my eight o'clock meeting to hear all the gory details of your weekend. I've been married for fifteen years. I am now living vicariously through you," Erin said as she brushed an imaginary piece of lint on her skirt. "So, I don't want to hear any vague 'oh we had a lovely time, blah blah blah'. I want all the details!"

Grinning at Erin's eagerness, Kate sat down and leaned back into her chair. "I don't know where to start, Erin. We talked, drank wine, took Mary to the beach, went out to dinner and the art gallery, went to a movie," Kate rambled. A wicked smile graced her lips as she continued. "And had lots, and lots, and lots of sex," Kate said wickedly.

"Yes, this is what I'm talking about!" Erin exclaimed. "I knew it. How much is lots and lots and lots?"

"Pretty much non-stop after Mary left for Georgie's," Kate

grinned.

"Ugh. You're so lucky. I don't remember marathon sex weekends. That's what happens when you have kids. No more marathon sex weekends. Hell, no more sex period!"

Kate grinned. "The moment I opened the door to him Friday night, it was like no time had passed since I saw him last," Kate said glancing out her office window.

"That scares you," Erin said softly.

Kate blinked and looked into Erin's eyes. "So much."

"Why?"

"Because it's so fast!" Kate stood and paced back and forth behind her desk. "Erin, we fell into bed with each other like we've been married for years. There was no awkwardness, no shyness." Kate glanced up and saw Erin's patented eye roll. "Hey! What's with the eye roll?"

"If I had something handy, I'd throw it at you," Erin said while slowly shaking her head. "Sit down, you're making me nervous." Erin waited until Kate was settled and then she speared her with a glare. "Brad's gone Kate," Erin said quietly.

Sucking in her breath, Kate's face drained of color. "You think I don't know that?"

"I know you know it. I watched you grieve for him. I continue to watch you grieve for him. When are you going to forgive yourself? He made the choice, Kate. He made *all* the choices. You have to let it go. You have to let *him* go. You deserve happiness and Edward seems like an amazing catch."

Kate's expression was bleak. "But what if it ends? What if he's not my happy ever after? It's not just me that I have to be concerned about anymore."

"Then you'll move on and find someone new. But I think the bigger and more important question is 'What if he is'?"

Two hours later, Kate was still mulling over that question. 'What if he is?' Erin was good at asking the questions. But Kate didn't have the answers. She liked Edward a lot. And if she was completely honest with herself, she was half in love with him already.

Sighing, she decided to put that alarming thought and all the questions out of her mind for the time being. She had a lot of work to do, and sitting here mulling over her personal life wasn't getting it done.

Edward's mind was moving in the same direction as Kate's as he flew across the ocean back to London. Their morning had been amazing, hell the whole weekend had been beyond amazing. Was it really possible, in real life, to feel a lasting connection with someone so fast? If he was going to take the plunge, he wanted it to last. He didn't want to be another in a long line of failed romances, gracing the covers of all the news rags.

The chiming of his blackberry drew him from his thoughts. He glanced at the screen and sighed. Back to the grind...

"Are you on your way back?" This from his assistant, James.

Typing fast and hoping James just wanted confirmation, Edward replied. "Yes. Expect to land around noon."

"Good. Producers not happy with delay."

"They'll get over it," Edward texted back.

"Not the best attitude to have at the beginning of a project, Edward."

Edward rolled his eyes and sighed. "I'm not going to apologize for taking an extra day."

"I'm just saying it might be wise to tone down your attitude."

"And I'm saying if it's that big a deal, they can find someone else. I don't need this grief, and I certainly don't need this project."

"Whoa. No grief, just giving you a head's up."

"Appreciate the head's up. And that's what I'm giving you as well."

"Noted. Are you coming straight to the studio?"

"Yes."

"Brilliant, I'll meet you there."

Edward tossed his blackberry onto the table, and poured himself some coffee. Sinking into the seat, Edward stared out the window as he drank the coffee. Five years. He'd been working straight for five years with no real breaks in between. A week here and there between projects didn't really constitute a vacation.

Maybe that's why his relationship with Kate was running so hot. Picking up his blackberry, he texted the one person he knew would be completely honest with him.

"Mum, you busy?"

"Never too busy to talk to you."

Edward smiled. "I'm on my way back from America. Headed to the studio. Join me for dinner tonight?"

"Love to. You ok?"

"Yes, just want to talk. I'll send a car for you around six.

Ok?"

"Yes. Fancy or normal?"

Edward chuckled. "Normal. Love you, Mum."

"Love you more. See you tonight."

He drained his coffee cup and set it down on the table. Leaning his head back, his eyes drifted closed. Better grab some sleep now before he entered the lion's den. He'll need his wits about him, especially if what James said was true and the producers were unhappy.

If his day could get worse, Edward didn't see how. He politely swerved his way through the throngs of people in the terminal. He ignored the surprised looks from people he passed and didn't look anyone in the eye. He didn't have time to get held up by an admiring fan, he was due at the studio in ten minutes. Unless there was a helicopter waiting for him in the parking lot, there was no way he'd make it on time. It wasn't what he needed, especially given James' warning earlier. Sighing deeply, he glanced at his watch again and groaned inwardly. Make that five minutes. Stepping outside of the terminal, he looked up and down for his car. Jason must have gotten held up in the parking garage. Edward pulled out his phone and quickly sent James a text to let him know he was running behind schedule. Shoving his phone back in his pocket, Edward started to pace as he waited for Jason to arrive with the car. He was distracted by his thoughts and didn't notice the small group of fans that were watching his every move.

"This is my lucky day! Mr. Kent, may I have a moment of your time?"

Edward glanced up and rolled his eyes. A reporter, he was wrong. His day could get worse. "I'm waiting on my car, I don't really have time for a chat."

"Just a couple of questions, while you wait for your car?" The reporter walked closer and stood just in front of Edward, blocking any chance of escape.

Edward drew himself up to his full height, his clear blue gaze settling on the reporter's face. He fixed a bored stare on his face and nodded slightly to the reporter. "And you are?"

"Brent, sir. From *The Moon*," he said proudly.

Edward shook his head, disgust rolling through him. A gossip rag, just wonderful. Anything he said would be twisted around until it barely resembled anything he said.

"Mr. Kent, is it true that you're just returning from America?"

"It is," Edward said carefully.

"Are you investigating a new project over there? Leaving us for the glam and glitz of Hollywood?"

Edward smiled. "My home is here, not Hollywood. Surely you know that?"

"You've been photographed several times with a new lady. She wouldn't happen to be the reason for your trip to America?"

Edward's demeanor transformed instantly. His muscles bunched, ready to fight. A cold light entered his eyes and a scowl replaced the bored smile on his face. He stepped forward, invading the reporter's personal space. "My personal life if my own. I don't answer questions relating to it for anyone, you should already know that."

Brent stepped back, a little bit of fear creeping along his skin. He cleared his throat before he continued. "Surely just a nibble, sir? Our readers want to know if England's most eligible bachelor is no longer eligible."

Edward smiled thinly. "No comment." He reached down and grabbed his bag. Wasting one last glance at the reporter, Edward moved to the curb. Jason pulled up right in front of him and Edward opened the door before Jason had a chance to come around and open it for him.

"Mr. Kent, please. Give me something to take back with me!" Brent begged before Edward could close the car door.

Edward started to close the door and then reconsidered. "If you were the last reporter on Earth, if my survival depended on you getting a sound bite, I'd still say No Comment."

With that he slammed the door and motioned for Jason to drive.

Brent watched the car drive off and cursed under his breath. "Thinks everything is about him and can't share. I'll show him. Somehow or another, I'll show him how it is. Scratch my back, and I'll scratch yours." Kicking at the curb, he turned around and headed back to the office. Mr. Kent wasn't going to like what was coming down the road. Not now, and certainly not later. He'd find out what was going on in America, and he'd certainly find out who the little filly was that Mr. Kent was so gone on. Nothing got by Brent for long. Nothing.

Chapter Nineteen

"Edward, over here."

He glanced up and saw James waving to him from across the lot. He waved and worked his way toward his assistant.

"James." Edward nodded and shook hands with him.

"Your trailer is over here," James said as he led Edward through a maze of trailers.

Stepping up into the trailer, Edward threw his coat onto the nearest chair. He walked over to the refrigerator and grabbed a bottled water.

After taking a long drink, he turned to James. "What's on the agenda?"

"First thing is a meeting with the director and writers. Starts in twenty minutes."

"Good, that gives me a few minutes to freshen up." Edward finished the water and put the empty bottle in the recycling bin. Turning, he headed to the restroom to freshen up and change his clothes, but stopped in his tracks when James spoke.

"So, what was so important that you had to delay your return?"

"A personal matter. Nothing you need to concern yourself with," Edward said tersely.

"I disagree," James argued with a bit of heat in his voice. "When *the* Edward Kent disappears for a whole weekend, it becomes my concern. Especially since people look to me to know every step you take."

Edward sighed. "Listen, I know we haven't worked together for long. Understand that my personal life is off-limits. I won't be discussing it with you or anyone."

A scowl appeared on James' face. "I'm not asking for all the gritty details, Edward. I'm asking for common courtesy. You were off having a brilliant time, I hope, and I was here trying to assure people that you were well, committed to this project, and not dead in some ditch."

Edward leaned against the wall and sighed. "I apologize, James. You're right, that was selfish and rude of me. I will do my best to ensure it doesn't happen again."

"Apology accepted."

Edward turned his back to James, but paused to drop a bomb before he went into the bathroom. "I need a holiday, James. Once this project is complete, I want you to clear six months off my calendar."

"Wh-what? Six months? Consecutive?"

Smiling to himself, Edward nodded. "A consecutive six months. I've been five years without a holiday, James. I'm burning out, and I don't think you want Edward Kent burning out on your watch. Do you?"

"No, sir. I don't. What about the Jane Austen period piece? That's your next project."

"Figure out a way to get them to graciously postpone. I'm sure you can handle it."

"Sir, six months? You're not going into rehab are you?"

Edward laughed and moved into the restroom. Speaking loudly, he replied, "Rehab, no. A holiday and spending time with family, yes. Make it happen, James."

He was running late for dinner. No one had been able to leave well enough alone. The director wasn't happy with a scene, so the writers fixed it. Then the actors weren't happy. Another fix, another argument. He understood everyone's need to be happy, but going over one scene for three hours was enough to drive him to the rehab James had suggested earlier.

Pulling out his blackberry, he quickly sent a text to his dinner date. "Mum, leaving studio now. Be there in fifteen. Writers, grrr. Sorry."

"Ok. I'm here at our usual table. Red or white?"

"Red, please. See you soon."

True to his word, he walked through the doors fifteen minutes later. He smiled when he saw his favorite maître'd standing by the podium. "Barnaby! How are you? How's your wife doing?"

"Mr. Kent, nice to see you. She's doing much better, thank you for asking. It was touch and go there for a bit, but she's on the mend. Doctors are saying full recovery."

Barnaby's wife had been stabbed on the tube. The person hadn't been caught and Barnaby's wife had been in the hospital for several weeks. Edward made a mental note to send more flowers and a card. "I'm glad to hear that. Give her my love."

"I will, enjoy your dinner."

Edward walked over to his table and leaned down to kiss his mother's cheek. "Mum, sorry I'm late. How are you?"

"Stop apologizing, Edward. It's fine. I don't mind cooling my heels for a few minutes. Besides, I've just returned from your Aunt's house and I'm still enjoying the peace and quiet," she laughed.

"And how is Aunt Imogen?"

"She's good. Busy. That's a woman you'd better not keep waiting!"

"Indeed, she'll box my ears!"

Laughing, Charlotte Kent scrutinized her son's face. As her only son, he held special place in her heart. She loved each of her three children, but Edward was near and dear to her heart. She suspected it was because he reminded her so much of his father. Daniel Kent had been a special man, and Edward was the same. Seeing nothing to cause her serious concern, she patted his hand. "How was America?"

"Well, to be honest, it was amazing. And scary."

He was interrupted by the waiter. After giving their order, Charlotte touched his hand to get his attention. "A woman?"

Smiling, he squeezed her hand. It was comforting to have someone who knew him so well. He nodded. "Yes. Her name is Kate. I met her about four months ago here in London. Chance meeting at Tempo in Mayfair. She was having dinner and asking the waiter about Pappagallo's. I sat with her and we fell into conversation. She went back to the States and when she returned last month, we went to dinner every night she was in town. Then she went home again and I got called back to Jamaica. We didn't speak for a month. I called her when I got back to London and it was like time had stood still for that month. I hopped on a plane and spent the weekend with her."

Grinning broadly, Charlotte clapped her hands. "That's lovely! But why are you scared?"

"I don't know? I feel like it should be harder. We should be going slower. We're both a bit scared. It feels like we've known each other forever and were just waiting for the right time to meet again."

"Edward, the saying 'too good to be true' doesn't apply to love."

Edward blanched. "Love? Mum, slow down. I've only known her a couple of months."

Sighing softly, Charlotte tutted. "Do you know how long I knew your father before I fell in love with him?"

Edward groaned and rolled his eyes. "An hour. Mum, you and Dad have told us this story a million times."

"It's not a work of fiction, Edward. It's not a movie or a script or a book. It's my life. It's real and it happened. An hour was all it took and I knew I wanted to spend the rest of my life with him. It's not inconceivable to think that couldn't happen to you."

"You don't think I'm crazy?"

"No, not in the least. In fact, I think it's wonderful that you've finally met someone you feel this strongly about. When do I get to meet her?"

Edward laughed. "Soon. She'll be here in about six weeks for work, but I'll be in Italy. She's planning to come back with Mary when I return."

"Who's Mary?"

"Her daughter."

Charlotte clapped her hands again. "Oh, a grand-baby! You melt my heart, Edward!"

"Mum! Don't get too attached yet," Edward warned. "What if it doesn't work? What if I'm wrong?"

"Edward, it's not like you to be so serious and negative." She reached for his hand again. "Love isn't something to be stressed about. It has a life of its own. A little weeding here and there, some water and lots of sun and fresh air. That's what it takes to have a beautiful garden of love and affection with someone. A wonderful story to tell your children and grandchildren."

"It feels so right, Mum. She's so amazing. She's kind and considerate, beautiful, a great sense of humor. She's devoted to Mary and is an amazing mother."

"She sounds like the perfect woman for you."

"She doesn't know about me, though."

"What? How could she have doubts as to the kind of person you are?"

Edward laughed. "No, not like that. I mean, she doesn't know I'm 'Edward Kent'," he explained, using air quotes when he said his name.

"How?"

"Well, I'm making some in-roads in America, but I'm not as famous there. I don't think she's made the connection."

"Do you think it'll matter?"

"I hope not. She's very private and I don't know how she'll feel about living in the public eye – something that will definitely happen if we take our relationship to the next level."

"Well, there's only one way to find out."

"True. I felt safer visiting her in America. There's less of a chance that I'll be recognized. Although, we've been photographed, a few times here and once there. I was able to brush off the ones she noticed."

"When they visit, will you be in London or out at the estate?"

"We'll go out to the estate. It's private and I won't have to worry about the paparazzi."

"You said she's bringing the baby?"

"Yes, Mary, but she's not really a baby. She's five and the sweetest little thing."

"Where's the father?"

"Died, about five years ago. I don't know the whole story. I think it's still pretty painful for her to talk about yet."

"Is she ready for this?"

"I'm not sure. And I don't know if she knows. I do know she's scared and worried at how fast we're moving," he said. He looked up with a mischievous grin. "I guess we'll just have to see how it grows."

Smiling, Charlotte patted his hand. "Yes. Take it a day at a time, but be sure to care for it. Otherwise it'll wither."

Ready to change the subject, Edward sipped his wine. "How are my sisters?"

"Oh, I have some news and I can't believe it took me so long to tell you! Meaghan is pregnant! But, you didn't hear that from me," Charlotte added sternly. The huge smile on her face lessened the effect her stern voice had.

"She is? That's bloody brilliant!" Edward was so pleased.

Meaghan and Rufus had been trying for seven years to get pregnant. "I have to call her. I'll take her to lunch this week. They must be over the moon."

Charlotte was shaking her head. "No. I mean, they are thrilled, but she's on bed-rest."

"What? Already? How far along is she?"

"Twelve weeks, but the doctors don't want anything to go wrong. They are taking all the precautions."

Edward nodded in understanding. Six miscarriages had taken their toll and he was of the same opinion. Do everything to keep her safe. "I'll go visit her this weekend. How's Izzy?"

"She's herself. Apparently she broke up with Nico, but that's not really any big upset. She's top of her class at University."

"Fabulous. And you, Mum," Edward asked as he placed his hand over hers. "How are you?"

Charlotte squeezed his fingers in understanding. "I'm fine. I have good days and bad days, like everyone else. I miss him, everyday." She paused to take a sip of water. "I'm thinking about taking a cruise this winter. Get away from the snow and cold."

They'd lost Daniel Kent six months ago to a heart attack. They'd all been to church together and were sitting down to lunch, when he collapsed next to the table. Edward had immediately started CPR, but it hadn't helped. The doctors said he had died before he even hit the floor. The wound was still raw and Edward tried to block all thoughts of his father. Their father had been a rock, the rock, of the family.

"Do you want company?"

"I would, but who would go with me?"

"Me. I told James to work out a six month break after this project."

"Are you serious? When was the last time you took some time off?"

"I think it's been about five years. I'm due, don't you think?"

"Indeed. Oh Edward, I would adore that, truly!"

"Then it's set." Edward pushed his plate away. "Dessert, Mum?"

"No thank you, I'm full. But I wouldn't mind some tea, please."

Edward ordered her tea and a glass of port for himself. "Thank you for having dinner with me, Mum."

"Thank you for inviting me. It makes my heart happy to

know you kids still need me."

"Always. You're our Mum."

"I want to meet your Kate when she comes to visit and I want to spoil little Mary. You'll tell me when they're coming?"

"Like I could keep it from you!"

Chapter Twenty

The time dragged by slowly in Kate's opinion. She and Edward spoke on the phone several times a week. During the week, he always called after Mary was in bed, ever conscious of how much the down time with Mary meant to her. On the weekends, he would call during the day so that he got the chance to talk to Mary. An ocean between them and still Mary had him wrapped around her tiny finger.

After Kate's talk with Erin about her relationship with Edward, she had decided a second opinion was warranted. Georgie had gotten Tim to agree to watch Mary and Kate had escaped with Georgie on an overnight heart-to-heart disguised as a spa getaway.

Georgie, having known more about Kate's life with Brad, was a little more cautious with her advice than Erin was. But in the end, their advice was similar in that the relationship wouldn't get anywhere unless Kate tried. Taking it one day at a time was the smartest solution, but not be so cautious as to ruin a good thing.

And that's what Kate was doing, taking it one day at a time. She looked forward to the phone calls with Edward. They spoke about almost everything. The one thing she wouldn't discuss on the phone was Brad. She felt that it was a conversation that should be done in person, where they could look into each other's eyes and know what was in their hearts.

She felt as if Edward was holding on to his own secret. She wouldn't push though, figuring he'd tell her when he was ready. Or maybe he was waiting to do the in-person conversation as well.

She was pretty nervous about meeting his mother, although she felt as if she knew her already. One of Edward's favorite topics was his family. He was devoted to them and she loved that about him. In fact, there wasn't much about him that she didn't love.

She'd spoken on the phone a few times with his sister, Meaghan. Poor girl was bored out of her mind on bed-rest. Kate couldn't fathom spending her whole pregnancy in bed.

Looking around the apartment, Kate tried to think of anything she'd forgotten to pack. "My mind is a blank."

"What do you mean?"

"I have no idea if I've packed everything we'll need."

"Well, let's start with the most important thing...do you have Mary's purple jaguar, otherwise known as 'Lovey'?"

Laughing, Kate nodded. "In my purse. It was the first thing I packed."

"Well then, you're all set. They have stores in England. I'm sure you can buy whatever you've forgotten."

"Good point." Kate picked up her purse. "Let's get out of here. Who knows how long it'll take to get through security."

Georgie walked over to help with the luggage. Frowning, she sent a questioning look to Kate. "You certainly didn't take after Mom in the packing department. This bag is so light, is it empty?"

"No, I didn't want to get hit with the heavy bag fee. I only packed enough for five days, I figure we can do laundry. Meaghan said she'd let me borrow a hairdryer and stuff. Their outlets are different anyway, so that saved me having to buy a converter too."

"Impressive. I can't pack like this. I have to have a couple options for each day. Who knows what I'll actually feel like wearing that day," Georgie laughed.

Shaking her head in amusement, Kate ushered them out the door and locked up.

"Thanks for the ride, Georgie."

"Not a problem. Those parking fees can get ridiculous." Georgie looked in the rear-view mirror at her niece. "Mary, are you excited about the plane ride?"

"Whee!"

Kate was so excited to be able to take this trip with Mary. They were going to have the best time.

Tired, hungry and at the very limit of her patience after trying to keep Mary occupied for the flight, Kate was a bundle of nerves. Of course, Murphy's Law would reign supreme keeping Mary awake the entire flight only to have her fall asleep ten minutes before the plane landed.

So overwhelmed with keeping Mary in her arms as she struggled with her luggage, she almost missed the tall man holding a sign with her name on it. He seemed familiar to her, but she couldn't place him. He was tall, nearly six feet, and muscular. Kate couldn't imagine he had an ounce of fat on his body. His eyes were silver and his nose slightly crooked. He had a scar running through his left eyebrow and was dressed head to toe in black. Stopping in front of him, she quietly spoke to him. "Excuse me, I'm Kate Walker."

The man inclined his head. "Ma'am, Mr. Kent sent me to pick you up. He got caught up at work." The man folded the sign and stooped to pick up her luggage.

"Thank you, err, what's your name?"

"Jason, ma'am."

"Thank you, Jason. Please, call me Kate." Relieved of the luggage detail, she shifted Mary into a more comfortable position and followed the man out of the airport. Pleasure lit up her face when they arrived at the car. A limousine. Kate had only ridden in one once. The day of her wedding. They'd ridden from the reception to the hotel. Jason held the door open for her and she slid inside, careful not to wake Mary.

"Kate, would you care to stop for some food? It's about an hour drive to Mr. Kent's estate."

"No, I have some snacks in my bag. Thank you for asking."

"My pleasure. Let me know if you need to stop."

Kate watched out the window as Jason pulled away from the curb. "Jason, did Edward say if he would be meeting us at his house?"

"I'm picking him up next. He'll be riding with you."

"Great!"

Twenty minutes later, Kate could barely contain her excitement when they pulled into the parking lot. She could see Edward waiting at the curb surrounded by people. She hoped they all weren't getting in the limo, there was no way

Mary would stay asleep with all that commotion.

As the limo glided to a stop, Jason exited and held open the door for Edward. "James, keep me updated on the cruise schedule and let me know asap when you hear about the final schedule. I'll be out at my estate, accessible by the normal means."

"Yes sir. Enjoy your week."

Edward slid into the car. "Hello beautiful!" He leaned over and kissed Kate. Sliding his hand over her hair, he looked deep into her eyes. "I've missed you." He dropped a light kiss on Mary's cheek. "I'm so glad you're both here."

"Thank you for the ride, Edward. Mary passed out as we were landing at Heathrow. I think we'd still be at the airport shuffling toward the rental car desk."

"I planned to be there, but got held up at work. I'm sorry. Today was a day from hell, but I think I made it that way. I was too keyed up about your arrival. I kept checking my watch every five minutes."

"I know what you mean. That was the longest flight in the history of flights," Kate smiled. "I'm so glad to be here. It's been torture to be away from you."

"Ah, Kate." He slid his arm along the back of the seat and pulled her close to his side. "Ditto."

They passed the time speaking softly about their days and catching up since their last phone call. Before they realized it, Jason was pulling into the driveway of Edward's estate.

"Wow, are we here already?"

"We are," Edward confirmed. "Welcome to my home, Kate."

Kate looked out the window and sucked in her breath. It was a mansion, literally. Three stories of grey stone. Kate thought it looked like something out of a Victorian era story. "Edward, it's, it's beautiful and huge." Kate's face turned slightly pink when she realized what she'd said.

Chuckling, Edward agreed. "When I come out here, my whole family usually shows up to visit. The good thing about this place being so huge is that we can all be in here and not see each other if we choose. But that's not usually the case."

"Is your family planning on visiting while I'm here?"

"Mum is planning to visit. Izzy is at University, she might come out on the weekend. Meaghan won't be, since she's on bed-rest. I thought perhaps we could go visit her one day this week, though. She'd really like to meet you in person."

"Of course, I'd love to meet her. And it doesn't bother me,

Edward. I was just curious."

"Well, it bothers me. I want you both to myself while you're here. Call me selfish."

Kate cupped his cheek. "You're not selfish, Edward. I don't think you could be, even if you wanted to. You're sweet and amazing and I'm so thankful for you."

Edward leaned toward her and stopped just as he was about to kiss her. "I'm humbled and touched that you feel that way." He touched his lips to hers, careful to keep it brief. They'd have time enough later to indulge.

"Sir." Jason said as he opened Edward's door. Edward got out of the limo and reached in to take Mary into his arms. She stirred slightly and he pressed her head onto his chest, soothing her with soft kisses on her forehead. Safe in his arms, she went back to sleep.

Kate gathered her purse and Mary's backpack and got out of the limo. Stretching, she groaned softly. Holding Mary for so long had made her muscles ache. As she looked around, she gaped at the sight before her. Edward's estate was massive. Perfectly manicured lawns and gardens. Giant trees that looked like they'd been there for hundreds of years. A huge willow stood in the middle of the driveway and Kate could imagine Edward climbing the tree as a child. She smiled to herself and followed Edward up the steps to the door.

Kate couldn't believe her eyes when the door was opened by a dour-faced man. He was tall and thin and looked to be at least ninety years old. "A butler? You have a for real butler? I didn't think they actually existed anymore."

Laughing, Edward nodded to the butler. "This is Henry. Henry, this is Kate and her daughter, Mary."

"Pleased to meet you, ma'am."

Kate stuck her hand out toward Henry. He gently took her hand and gave it a quick shake. "Please, call me Kate."

"As you wish," he said. He turned toward Edward. "Mrs. White will be right down. She noticed the sleeping child and ran up to turn down the blankets in the room."

"Oh, that was so kind of her," Kate said. Unsure what to do with herself, Kate surreptitiously glanced around the foyer.

Edward nodded toward a table in the foyer. "You can set your purse and bag down on that table, if you like, Kate."

Kate walked over to the table and set her things down. As Kate turned to walk back to Edward's side, a woman ran down the stairs and exploded into the foyer. There really was no other word for it. The amount of energy this woman radiated could light up all of England for years.

"Edward!" Mrs. White exclaimed quietly, giving him a peck on the cheek. "So glad you're here, boy! Let me see that sleeping child. Oh my, she's so sweet. Hello, you must be Kate. I'm Mrs. White, Edward's housekeeper. You must be exhausted after your trip. Come, I'll show you to your rooms and you can get freshened up. Edward, is your Mum coming for dinner tonight?" Mrs. White asked as she led them up the stairs.

Kate blinked. This woman was a whirlwind, and Kate didn't know if she'd be able to keep up with her.

"Not that I'm aware of, Mrs. White, but then you'd know better than I would anyway," Edward chuckled.

"Don't be cheeky, my boy. It's not becoming. I spoke with your Mum this morning, but she wasn't sure if it would be a good idea for her to come out. She mentioned it might be better for her to come tomorrow what with the long trip and the time difference."

"That's a good point. I'll call her in a few minutes after I discuss it with Kate."

"Kate, here is your room," Mrs. White gestured. "The child's is next door – there's a connecting door between your rooms. I thought it would make you both feel more comfortable to have that immediate access."

"Thank you, Mrs. White. That was considerate of you." Kate entered her room and couldn't believe her eyes. The room was huge and beautiful. Done in cream, rose and gold, the windows overlooked a lovely garden at the back of the estate. The lovely scent of roses in full bloom drifted in through the open windows. The bed was a huge four-poster complete with sheer curtains surrounding it. She slowly walked around her room, touching the table and the bedding as she went. She finally came to a stop in front of the windows, amazed at the view.

She jumped when Edward touched her shoulder. "Do you like your room?"

"Like it? I love it. It's beautiful, thank you." She turned to face him and reached up to place a light kiss on his cheek.

"I put Mary in her bed. She's still sound asleep. Will she sleep long?" Edward asked with a wicked gleam in his eye.

"I have no idea, to be honest." Kate rested her head against his chest. "Edward, I figured you were rather well-to-do...but this," Kate gestured around the room and pointed outside. "This is so much more than doing well."

"Does it matter, Kate?"

"No, of course not. I mean, a little warning would have been nice. I thought the limo was a special thing, I didn't realize that it was your actual everyday car." Kate smiled so that he would know she wasn't criticizing him.

"Kate, you're so special to me."

Kate reached up and brushed his hair off his forehead. "I know, and you're special to me too. I just feel a little lost, is all. I wasn't expecting Buckingham Palace, Edward."

Edward laughed. "Buckingham Palace is four times the size of this place."

Kate whistled. "Oh! Hmm, I guess you're not doing that well, then."

Laughing, Edward spun her around. "Let me show you around."

"One second, let me get the monitor out and plugged in. In case she wakes up."

Edward hooked the monitor to his pants and they quietly left Mary's room. "First, I'll show you how to get to my room...just in case you need me in the night."

Kate giggled, and followed him into a room that was at least twice the size of hers. Her whole apartment back home would have fit in his bedroom. Edward's room was decorated in dark blues and grays.

The view from his room was beyond compare. Just below the windows was yet another garden. The gardenias were in full bloom and the scent wafted up through the open windows. Kate could barely make out the stables off to the right, and toward the left was the distinct sparkle of water. "Do I see water out there?"

"Yes, there's a huge lake on this property. Would you like to go swimming or boating?"

"Yes, to both!" Kate said eagerly. Mary loved to play in the water and Kate could think of nothing so relaxing as sailing around the lake.

"We'll do that as well. We are going to have a very busy and fun week!"

"Will you be going to work during the day, Edward?" Kate asked as they left Edward's room and moved on in the tour of the house.

"Not unless it's absolutely unavoidable. I have the week off to spend with you lovely ladies."

"Truly? Oh, Edward, that is so wonderful!"

Edward reached for her hand and linked their fingers

together. He quickly showed her the rest of the bedrooms on the floor and then they moved down the stairs to see the rest.

Kate was astounded. There was a formal dining room, a small ballroom, a library, a sitting room, a den that Edward said he used as his office, the kitchens and no fewer than three half-baths. "What do you do with all this space?"

"Nothing much. This house dates back to the early seventeen hundreds. It's been redecorated and updated a few times since then, but it's essentially the same. My dad's family lived close to here and I can remember passing this house whenever we would come to visit my grandparents. I used to fantasize about living here and I'd dream about the fancy parties I'd host and pretend about being "lord of the manor". About three years ago, the owner passed away and he had no family. It was on the market for about twenty minutes before I snatched it up. I imagine someday when I get married, I'll fill these rooms with the laughter of children. But for now, it's a nice retreat when I need away from the hustle and bustle of the city."

"It's a beautiful home, Edward."

Raising her hand to his lips, Edward lightly brushed a kiss against her knuckles. "I'm happy you're here, Kate."

"Mama?" They heard over the monitor.

"And she's awake!" Kate said. "Let's go get her before she decides to wander off on her own. It'll take weeks to find her in this place," Kate joked.

They walked up the stairs together, and when Kate pushed open the door to her room, they found Mary sitting in the middle of the floor. "Hi baby, did you have a good nap?"

"Where are we, Mama?"

Kneeling in front of Mary, Kate brushed her hair back from her forehead. "We're at Edward's home. Remember we flew in the airplane?"

Mary lifted her face to see Edward and a beautiful smile broke out on her face. "Edward!" Mary squealed. She stood up, walked over to Edward and lifted her arms. The universal sign for "pick me up". Edward obliged and easily lifted her into his arms.

"Well, I see who the favorite is now," Kate smiled as she spoke.

"Well, that's only because she knows about my h-o-r-s-e-s." Edward spelled.

Kate laughed and tickled Mary on the belly. "I'm glad you spelled that because otherwise we'd be out there right now."

"Mama, I'm so hungry!" Mary said in between giggles.

"Alright, let's go feed your belly."

Chapter Twenty-One

"Where's my new grand-baby?" Charlotte asked the room at large the following afternoon.

Kate and Edward were in the sitting room enjoying some down time as Mary took a much needed nap. They'd been out riding horses all morning and between the excitement of the activity and the fresh air, Mary had been done in. Kate had found a new mystery series in Edward's vast library and was laying on the couch, her head in Edward's lap, reading the first book of the series. Edward was rubbing Kate's head as he channel surfed, looking for a cricket game.

Kate and Edward, startled by the appearance of his mother, jumped a foot in the air. Kate dropped her book on the floor and almost followed it when Edward jumped to his feet.

"Mother!" Edward said a little too loud. "I thought you wouldn't be here until later," he said sheepishly as he helped Kate to her feet.

"That much is apparent," Charlotte said dryly. She walked over to Kate and presented her hand. "You must be Kate? I've heard so much about you."

Kate put her hand in Charlotte's and was surprised when the woman pulled Kate into a hug. "All good, I hope?" Kate asked in a strangled voice. Her anxiety levels were through the roof. She hadn't prepared herself for meeting his mother until dinner time.

Kate shuddered. Here she was, laying on the couch, her head in Edward's lap. How embarrassing! This was his mother. The man practically worshipped the ground this woman walked on. Kate couldn't envision a worse first meeting.

"Absolutely, my dear girl," Charlotte assured her. "He adores you, and I can see why."

"Thank you," Kate said, blushing. Not really sure what to do with herself, Kate sat back down on the couch. It wasn't her house, or her place, to offer refreshments and Edward wasn't exactly being the 'Host with the Most' right now.

"So, where's my new grand-baby?" Charlotte sat down in one of the overstuffed chairs.

Kate glanced at Edward in confusion. Who in the world was this woman talking about? Edward hadn't mentioned a new family member, at least not that Kate could recall.

"Taking a nap," Edward said finally breaking out of his stupor. "We took Mary horseback riding this morning and she was tuckered out when we got back."

"Yes, that'll wear them out for sure," Charlotte agreed.

"I'm sure she'll be up soon," Kate said, desperately hoping it was true. It was wrong of her to use her child as a buffer, but she couldn't help it. Sending telepathic signals up to her sleeping child, she prayed they shared that special gift.

"Oh, let the child sleep. I'm sure she's still catching up from the time difference," Charlotte said. "Besides, this will give us a chance to visit and get to know each other better."

Kate paled. Why was she so nervous about meeting this woman?

Charlotte chuckled. "Edward, your Kate looks nervous to meet me. What have you told her about me?"

"What?" Kate paled further. "No, he's only had the nicest things to say about you!" She said quickly.

Edward laughed and sitting down next to Kate on the couch, he linked his fingers with hers. "Mother, please."

"What? I'm just trying to get to know this girl that has stolen your heart."

"Mother!"

"Alright, alright!" Charlotte raised her hands in surrender. She sighed and stood. "I'm going to get some tea, I'll be right back."

Kate watched her go and felt a pang of regret. Could their first meeting have gone any worse? Rising to her feet, Kate excused herself. "I'll go help your mother bring in some refreshments."

"You don't have to do that, Kate. She'll rope one of the maids into helping her bring them in."

"Oh," Kate paused. Sighing, she dropped back onto the couch. "Oh, Edward, I totally screwed that up."

"What do you mean?"

Kate gestured wildly with her arms. "This first meeting. I was so nervous about meeting her, I stumbled over my words. I hadn't gotten myself psyched up yet because I thought you said she would be here later." Kate stared at the doorway. "That was your mother!" Kate dropped her head in her hands and wanted to cry.

Edward scooted closer to Kate and draped his arm around her shoulders. "Kate, honey, it's nothing to worry about. Mum is very laid back, I'm sure she didn't notice anything amiss."

"She'd have to be blind, Edward! Look at me, I'm a mess. I'm covered in hair from the horse, I have mud on my pants, my hair is windblown and messy, I'm not wearing any makeup. And, I was laying in your lap. I'm sure I look as frightful as I sounded. Your mother probably thinks I'm some crazy person that's attached herself to you because you were so nice as to show me some attention one night."

"Kate, you look beautiful to me. As always. A little horsehair and mud isn't going to change that," Edward said as he hugged her close to his side. "Let me tell you a secret about my mum. She's sneaky and stealthy, especially when it comes to the well-being of her children but she has the best heart," Edward confided. "To be honest, she probably had been standing at the doorway for a minute or two taking in the scene we had presented."

Kate sighed. She was totally overreacting, and she had no idea why. It wasn't usually like her to lose this much of her confidence. Taking a deep breath, she slowly exhaled. "She did that grand entrance on purpose?"

"Yes. Most likely she wanted to see what you were like when taken by surprise. Mum's not overly fond of people who suck up to her because she's my mum. I'm sorry, I should have warned you," Edward said.

"No, it's ok. I understand," Kate said and smiled.

"Just relax and be yourself. I have one of the coolest mums

out there. She'll love you!" Edward smiled.

"Alright, here's the tea. I brought some for everyone," Charlotte said as she walked through the door. She was carrying three glasses and Kate jumped up to help her. Kate carefully extracted two glasses from Charlotte and passed one to Edward. Sitting back down next to him, she sipped the tea.

Frantically wracking her brain, Kate couldn't come up with one topic to discuss. What did one discuss when first meeting their boyfriend's mother?

"Kate, Edward says you work for Eclipse Fashion?"

"Yes, for about five years now. I absolutely love my job."

"How did you get into fashion?"

"Well, after Mary was born, I decided to go back to work part-time. When I went in for the interview, they informed me that the part-time position had already been filled and they wanted me for the full-time position. The benefits and salary were too good to pass up. They have a daycare facility in the building, so Mary and I get to see each other during the day. It's amazing!"

"What do you do?"

"Well, now I'm in charge of the marketing for the current product line, but when I first started I was an executive assistant. I went back to school and got a marketing degree and a few months ago I got promoted."

"Congratulations!"

"Thank you! This company has really been a blessing." Kate sipped her tea. "How's Meaghan?"

"Oh, she's doing as well as can be expected. She's bored. She wants to be up shopping for the baby and putting the nursery together," Charlotte sighed. "It's going to be a long nine months."

"Mum, isn't there anything we can do to help?" Edward asked.

"Well, of course there is. And we will. But that's not the point. Meaghan wants to do it herself."

Kate nodded her head in agreement. "She's right. It's called nesting, and it's instinctual and annoying. I remember the feeling," Kate shuddered as she thought back. She and Georgie had done most of the work on Mary's nursery once Brad had shut down. Georgie had insisted that Kate have no part in the painting and wallpapering, and it had driven Kate crazy. And when it was time to put the furniture together, Georgie had insisted that Kate let Tim do it. To Kate it had felt like it wasn't really happening unless she could put her hands on the project.

Edward shook his head. "That's above my education level," he laughed.

Kate settled back into the couch and her heart lightened when Edward draped his arm around her shoulders again. She liked that he wasn't afraid to show affection in front of his mother.

They passed an hour chit-chatting and Kate realized that she had relaxed and was actually enjoying herself. Kate was surprised to find out that Edward hadn't actually seen his mother in a few weeks. Charlotte had been up in Scotland helping her sister with the gardening and such. Charlotte regaled them with stories from her travels and caught Edward up with all the gossip from the family.

"Mommy?"

Mary stood in the doorway clutching her lovey. Kate smiled and went over to hug Mary. "How was your nap?"

"Good. I'm hungry," Mary said.

"I bet. All that fresh air is good for an appetite!"

"I'll go get her something from the kitchen. You two cuddle on the couch," Edward said.

Kate walked Mary over to the couch and sat down. "Thank you Edward," Kate said as she smiled at him. "Mary, I'd like to introduce you to someone very special." Kate gestured toward Charlotte. "This is Edward's mother, Ms. Charlotte. Would you say hello?"

"Hello," Mary said shyly.

"Well, hello, Mary. It's so nice to meet you!" Charlotte sent a beaming smile in Mary's direction. "I hear you went riding on the horses this morning. I bet that was fun!"

Nodding her head rapidly, Mary glanced at her mother. "Can we do it again?"

Smiling, Kate nodded. "Of course. But let's wait a bit. Edward is getting you a snack and we're visiting with Ms. Charlotte."

"Ok." Mary's face fell but just then Edward returned with a snack of apples and peanut butter and a smile lit up her face again.

"Thank you," Mary said as Edward handed her the plate and a napkin.

"You're most welcome."

Charlotte waited for Mary to finish her first apple slice before asking her another question. "Mary, which horse did you ride this morning?"

"Thunder! Edward let me ride with him on his big horse. He was so beautiful, Ms. Charlotte!"

Everyone listened as Mary recounted the morning's adventure. They had roamed all over Edward's property, through the trees and out on the pasture. They had stopped and picked wildflowers and Kate had made a daisy crown for Mary. The weather had been cool this morning, so they had skipped the lake, but Edward promised to take them out there in a day or two when the weather warmed up.

"Sounds like quite the adventure, little Mary. Are you enjoying your trip to London?"

Mary nodded having stuffed another apple in her mouth.

"Edward, will you be going into the City at all this week?" Charlotte asked.

"No, probably not. We're planning to visit with Meaghan tomorrow and then hopefully make a day of it at the lake. And I think Izzy is coming down on Saturday," Edward explained.

"Really, Izzy is coming down?"

"Well, she said she was. Nothing is ever in stone where she's concerned. If she doesn't it's no big deal," Edward said glancing at Kate in question.

"Right. I'm in London every few weeks. It's nice to just enjoy the peace of the countryside," Kate said.

"Mum, are you staying the week?"

"Only if it's not an intrusion. I'd love to get to know your girls and relax myself before heading back up to help your Aunt or over to Meaghan's to help there. I'm sure Rufus is pulling out what's left of his hair."

"It's never an intrusion, Mum. I had Mrs. White fix up your room, in case you wanted to stay," Edward said.

"Thank you, dear."

"How about a walk in the gardens?" Kate suggested. "Mary is finished with her snack and after such a long nap, she'll never sit still for long."

"Perfect, I could use some fresh air," Charlotte said.

Dinner that evening was a fun affair. The cook had prepared tacos for dinner after finding out it was Mary's favorite dinner. Charlotte had informed them all that it was her first time eating a taco. She had quickly fallen in love with the food.

Mary was seated next to Charlotte. The two of them had bonded so quickly during the walk in the garden. Charlotte had taken time to introduce Mary to all the different flowers in the garden and then allowed Mary to pick a small bouquet for her room. After the walk, the two of them retreated to the kitchen to trim the stems and put the flowers in a vase. Then they'd gone up to Mary's room to find the perfect place. They had settled on the bedside table. Mary explained that she'd be able to smell the flower smell better if it was next to her bed.

After that, Mary and Charlotte had spent time reading books and playing games. They all had retreated back to the sitting room in much the same way they'd been when Charlotte had arrived. Kate was laying on the couch reading and Edward was watching a cricket game. It had been a lovely afternoon and it warmed Kate's heart to see Mary interacting so well with Charlotte.

Kate's own mother was fond of Mary, and Kate never doubted her love for Mary. But Barbara never got down on the floor to play with Mary as Charlotte had done with the board games.

After dinner, Charlotte offered to give Mary her bath before bed. Kate couldn't say no, the two of them were like peas in a pod. Their love of tacos cementing their new relationship.

"Come with me, Kate. There's something I've been dying to do since you got here," Edward said as Charlotte and Mary disappeared up the stairs.

"Where to, Edward?"

"It's a surprise," Edward said as he winked at her.

Shrugging, Kate nodded and followed Edward. He led her back into the sitting room. He lowered the lights and picked up a remote. He pressed a couple of buttons and the soft music of Beethoven filled the room.

"Dance with me?" Edward said as he held his hand out toward Kate.

Charmed, Kate placed her hand in his. "I'd love to," Kate said.

Edward pulled her close and Kate rested her head on his chest. They moved as one to the music. The lights were dim, the music just loud enough to envelope them in their own bubble. Kate closed her eyes and let the moment take her away.

Chapter Twenty-Two

"Edward! You came!"

"Of course we came, Meaghan. Kate's been bugging me all week to see you!"

Kate elbowed Edward as she made her way over to Meaghan. Grasping her hands, she kissed Meaghan's cheek. "It's so good to meet you," Kate gushed. "This is my daughter, Mary."

"Hello, Mary! How are you doing?"

"Good," Mary smiled and placed her hand on Meaghan's stomach. "Wow! You're belly is big, how many babies do you have in there?"

Meaghan laughed, eyes twinkling. "Well now, I'm glad you asked. They tell me there are two babies in my tummy!"

Gasping, Kate clapped her hands and Edward kissed his sister's temple.   "Congratulations, Meaghan!"   Kate exclaimed.

"That's brilliant, Pip! When did you find out? Does Mum know?"

"No, Mum doesn't know, so please don't tell her. She said she's coming this weekend and I want to surprise her. We found out Monday."

"I'll do my best not to spill your beans, but you know how

Mum is," Edward grinned. "So, what have you been doing to keep yourself occupied, Pip?"

"Whining. Complaining. Perusing the internet for baby items. Driving Rufus crazy," Meaghan listed.

"Where is the old boy?" Edward asked.

"Knowing you were on the way, he escaped the madness to do some shopping. We're out of just about everything," she explained.

"It's a beautiful day outside, Meaghan. Are the lounge chairs out on the patio?"

"They should be, but if they aren't, they'll be in the shed."

"I'll go check and bring them out if need be. You should get some fresh air."

"I would adore it, thank you," Meaghan beamed.

"Point me in the direction of your kitchen and I'll get some refreshments ready to bring out with us," Kate offered.

"It's down the hall to the left. I doubt we have much, but help yourself. Rufus should be back soon with reinforcements."

"I'll be right back," Kate said. "Mary, will you keep Ms. Meaghan company?"

"Sure, Mommy!"

Kate helped Mary climb up on the bed and made sure they were comfortable before heading to the kitchen. She opened the fridge door and was a tad surprised to find it mostly empty. Meaghan had mentioned they were out of most everything, but Kate hadn't believed she'd been serious.

Next she went to the pantry and found a similar situation. Sighing to herself, she perused what was there and found enough odds and ends to put a light snack together. Buried deep on the bottom shelf, she found some instant lemonade mix and pulled that out too.

Kate sliced up some apples, cut some cheese into squares, laid out some crackers and made the lemonade. By the time she'd finished putting the food together, Edward had prepared the chairs outside. He was just lifting Meaghan to move her outside when she emerged from the kitchen.

"Perfect timing!" Kate said. "Mary, can you get the door for Edward, please?"

"Sure!" Mary ran ahead and opened the door wide, holding it until both Edward and Kate had gone through.

"Thank you, Mary," Meaghan said.

"You're welcome," Mary replied.

"Oh, Meaghan! It's beautiful out here!" Kate exclaimed.

The grass was lush and went on forever. The yard was level and dotted with a few oak trees. At the very end of the yard, at least a quarter mile away, she could just make out the sparkling water of a small pond.

"Thank you! Mum would love to get her hands on my yard and fill it with flowers, like she's done at Edward's house. But I keep refusing her," Meaghan sighed. "Don't get me wrong, I love flowers. But I don't have the time or the love to devote to them. Besides, I love the peacefulness of just the grass and trees."

"You know she'll wear you down eventually, Pip," Edward laughed.

"She can, but only if she's going to oversee their care."

"Mommy, can I run around?"

"Sure, just stay where I can see you."

"Meaghan, is the tire swing still up?"

In the middle of taking a sip of lemonade, Meaghan nodded.

"Come on, Mary. I'll push you on the swing."

Kate watched the two of them amble off, enjoying the view and the special bond that had grown between them.

"They look cute together," Meaghan observed.

Kate nodded. "Mary really adores him. My father spends some time with her, but it's my brother-in-law that really helps me out with the "dad" stuff. I don't know what I'd do without Tim and my sister."

"They don't have children?"

"No, unfortunately. They tried for years but nothing came of it. It's sad because they both would make such amazing parents."

"I know. I was really worried that we'd never have luck. This was our last IVF, I still can't believe it worked this time," Meaghan said.

"Would you have tried adoption if it hadn't worked out?"

"Yes. We both wanted to try everything we could to have our own babies first. But if it hadn't worked out, we would definitely adopt. In fact, when these babies are older, we'll probably adopt. Rufus and I have always wanted a big family. He has four brothers and three sisters. And while our family is small in comparison, we have a lot of cousins. I'm sure Edward has mentioned Aunt Imogen's brood," Meaghan laughed.

"Oh yes!"

"Well, I've always enjoyed the chaos that reigns there when

everyone is home. It's loud, boisterous and amazing. The air is thick with love, secrets and memories. I want that for our family."

"It sounds wonderful," Kate said.

"It is," Meaghan nodded enthusiastically. "Do you want more children, Kate?"

"I don't know," Kate said honestly. "Mary just turned six and I'm so far past the bottles, diapers and sleepless nights. She's pretty independent now and I'm not sure if I could go back," Kate explained.

"Hmm."

"When Brad died, I never expected to be here again. Until recently, I planned to be on my own for the rest of my life, focused on Mary. I'd accepted it and was at peace with it. I don't know, I guess we'll see what happens. If it's meant to be, it's meant to be," Kate said.

"What's this? Serious conversations on such a bright and beautiful day?"

Kate and Meaghan whipped their heads around to the sound of a new voice. A young woman stood framed in the door. Her pale blond hair, cut pixie short, made one focus on the twinkling cornflower blue eyes. She was tiny and couldn't have weighed more than a sack of flour. Her hot pink capri pants, black v-neck t-shirt and flip-flops with gerbera daisies attached to the toe strap, led Kate to believe she was a stylish young woman. Kate thought she was adorable.

"Izzy! What are you doing here?"

"I'm not allowed to take a day off and visit my whale of a sister?" Izzy laughed, walking out onto the patio and leaning over to kiss Meaghan's cheek.

"Oh you brat," Meaghan joked. "I'm not a whale yet, but I will be!"

"How big are you going to get?" she asked as she sat down at the bottom of Meaghan's lounge chair.

"Twice as big as normal," Meaghan said.

"Twins?! Are you having twins?" Izzy clapped and covered her mouth.

"Yes! Isn't it fantastic?" Meaghan asked beaming.

"Oh Meaghan! I'm so thrilled for you," Izzy leaned over and gently hugged her sister.

A huge smile lit up Izzy's face and Kate thought she was radiant.

"You must be Edward's Kate," Izzy said as she turned her head toward Kate.

"I am. It's so nice to meet you!"

Izzy glanced at Meaghan. "Have you interrogated her yet?"

Meaghan smiled. "No, not yet. I didn't think it would be right to do it without you."

Kate blinked. "Interrogate me? Are you the two wicked sisters?"

Meaghan and Izzy laughed. "No, but I think I like you already," Izzy said.

Meaghan and Izzy exchanged looks and then pinned Kate with their twinkling eyes.

"Do you like shopping?" Izzy asked.

Kate laughed. "Yes, of course."

"Do you like shoes?" Meaghan asked.

Kate twisted her foot up for inspection. She was wearing black and white polka dot heels. "I do."

"Well, I do like her taste in shoes," Izzy said to Meaghan.

"Do you like day trips to the spa?"

"Absolutely. And I hear that you both have trained Edward well. He's in favor of spa days!"

"It took a lot of work to bring Edward up to par. We want to make sure you don't undo all our hard work!" Izzy said smiling.

"Oh, I wouldn't dream of it," Kate replied.

"Do you like the theater?" Meaghan asked, bringing them back to the subject at hand.

"What I've seen of it so far, yes."

"What do you mean?" Meaghan asked.

"Well, I've only seen two plays. Both with Edward. And they've been amazing. I'm sure with more 'training' I could become quite attached," Kate explained.

Meaghan and Izzy exchanged another glance and after a second nodded their head slightly.

Izzy turned her bright eyes on Kate. "Welcome to our family!"

Kate smiled. Oh, she was going to get along just fine with his sisters.

"So, where's this little girl I've heard so much about?" Izzy asked.

"Mary and Edward are playing at the tire swing," Meaghan told her.

Izzy popped up and started walking. "I'm going to surprise him!"

Kate watched Izzy go and marveled at her energy and enthusiasm for life. "She's amazing," Kate breathed.

"That's a word for it. Usually I use 'whirlwind' when I describe her," Meaghan laughed.

They passed the day with lots of talking, enjoying the sunshine and warm weather. Kate and Edward took Mary down to the pond for some fishing while Meaghan took a nap. Izzy helped Rufus put the groceries away and then they both made a wonderful dinner of grilled steaks, baked potatoes and salad.

No one wanted the day to end, but Izzy needed to get back to school and Edward, Kate and Mary had an hour drive back to his house.

"Thank you for coming out and spending the day with me," Meaghan said as they gathered around her bed to say their goodbyes.

"It was such a pleasure! I promise to call you when I get home," Kate said.

"Good, our chats keeps me going. And they give poor Rufus a break!" Meaghan laughed.

"Can you call more often, please?" Rufus joked.

Laughing, Kate nodded her head. "I'll do my best."

"Keep those babies safe," Izzy said. "I'll call you tomorrow after class."

"I will. Drive safe." Meaghan reached up for a hug.

"Talk to you soon, Pip," Edward said. "Rufus, let me know if you need anything," Edward said as he shook hands.

Kate ushered Mary out the door, followed by Edward and Izzy.

"Lovely to have met you both," Izzy said as she hugged Mary. "Keep practicing your fishing, Mary. Maybe next time you'll catch us some dinner!"

Mary laughed. "I'll get Mom to fill up the bathtub."

Kate spluttered. "Uh, no I don't think so. Ew, no fish in my tub!"

"Where's your sense of adventure, Kate?" Edward asked.

"It stops at shoe shopping," Kate replied.

"I like that!" Izzy said. "Okay, well I'm off. Bye everyone!" Izzy waved as she walked over to her car.

Edward helped Kate and Mary into his car and they drove off, waving at Izzy when she took off like a dart down the driveway.

"Argh!" Edward said. "She drives like the devil!"

"She's fabulous. Both of them are. I really enjoyed today,"

Kate said.

"Me too. I forget sometimes how much I love them and enjoy them," Edward said.

"It's easy to do. Life has a funny way of doing that."

"Can we go to the lake tomorrow?" Mary asked from the backseat.

"You better believe it," Edward said.

"Yes!" Mary said as she pumped her fists in the air. "Best vacation ever!"

Kate and Edward smiled at each other. "Indeed," Kate whispered.

Chapter Twenty-Three

The next day they spent the morning at the lake, enjoying the water and each other's company. Charlotte had joined them for a little while, sitting on the beach with Kate while Edward and Mary played in the water.

Charlotte and Mary had gone to bed early. The exercise and sun making them ready for sleep earlier than usual.

Kate and Edward were curled up on the couch in the library, sipping wine. The windows were open allowing for an occasional breeze to blow through the room. A small fire was crackling in the fireplace, more for the comfort of it than a need for warmth.

"Kate, there's something I need to discuss with you," Edward said quietly as he stared into the fire.

Kate turned her head toward him and waited patiently for him to continue.

"When I told you that I work in the entertainment industry, I wasn't lying. I wasn't completely truthful, though. With the way I feel about you, I know I need to give you the whole truth," he hesitated again.

Kate gently cupped his cheek with her hand. "It can't be that bad, Edward. Just tell me."

Edward pressed his face deeper into his hand. "I know, but

things will change when I tell you this. And I don't want them to." He turned his face into her hand and kissed her palm. He took her glass of wine and set it with his on the table. He gently tugged her up his body so that she was now laying half on him with the couch behind her back. Leaning his head back along the armrest, he continued. "I'm an actor. Here in Europe, I'm pretty popular and I'm starting to make some inroads in America."

Kate sighed and rubbed her cheek against his chest. "Well, that explains it," Kate said.

"Explains what?" Edward asked.

"Your version of Buckingham Palace here," Kate said.

Edward laughed. "Really, that's all you have to say?"

"What were you expecting?"

"I don't know. Not a joke, that's for sure," he paused collecting his thoughts. "I guess I thought you might be upset because I kept it from you, or irritated about the inconvenience it'll cause when everyone finds out about you."

"I'm not upset that you kept it from me. I can understand why you did. I imagine being as famous as you are requires a certain cautiousness when you meet new people."

Edward was at a loss for words. "You're amazing, Kate."

Kate shook her head. "What do you mean, specifically, about the inconvenience?"

Edward sighed. "Well, I've been considered quite the eligible bachelor for a few years now. Once the press finds out I'm seeing someone, you'll have to contend with paparazzi trying to photograph you all the time. Reporters will be calling you. I can keep your name out of the network for a while, but eventually someone will talk and they'll learn your name. This will also put Mary in front of the camera as well," Edward said cautiously.

"Is there anything we can do to minimize the chances?"

"Well, we can spend time at your apartment. We can hide out here at the house. And we can charter a private plane for trips back and forth. But eventually, we'll be snapped together again."

"What?" Kate interrupted. "What do you mean, *again*?"

"Remember the flash of light when we were dining at The Mews?"

"Yes..."

"It was a photographer. They get paid for pictures of me and they were published here in London," Edward explained.

"My face has been splashed on your magazines?"

"And the newspapers." Edward reached behind him to the table and retrieved the magazine, *The Moon*, which had photographs of the two of them kissing at the show of *Kiss Me, Kate*. Opening it to the right page, he showed her the pictures.

"This was months ago," Kate said, shocked.

"I know. I bought the magazine when it came out. Look at the cover." Edward quickly flipped the magazine closed so she could see it.

The color drained from Kate's face as her brain processed what she saw. It was a grainy close up picture of the two of them kissing in the box of The Old Vic's theater. The caption under the photograph was undeniably rude.

Edward Kent hide here!
Actor caught snogging mystery woman at premiere of show.

Kate hid her face in his chest, embarrassment washing through her.

"I'm sorry, Kate. I know it's a lot to process. I've lived with this for a long time, and have had a lot of time to come to terms with the intrusion. I'll do my best to shield you from them, but they are relentless."

"I know that," Kate sighed. "My main concern is Mary. I don't want her face or her life splashed across magazines and papers. That's hard enough to deal with as an adult."

Edward rubbed her back and kissed the top of her head. "I don't want to lose you or Mary."

Lifting her face to look into his eyes, Kate smiled at him. "Oh Edward, I don't want that either. This is who you are and this is your life. We'll make this work somehow."

Squeezing her tight, Edward released a breath he wasn't aware he'd been holding. "I'll get in touch with my publicist and see if there's anything that can be done to keep Mary out of the focus," Edward promised.

"That would make me feel so much better," Kate said gratefully. Running her fingers over his chest, Kate decided now was as good a time as any to give Edward a head's up on her own secrets. "While we're being open with each other, I guess it's my turn to tell you a story..."

"Only if you want to, Kate. No pressure," Edward assured her.

"You've been so patient. But I'm sure you're wondering and my past will definitely be a headline story when they dig it up," Kate's laugh was forced. "I met Brad on the worst day of my life..."

Kate told Edward of the attack in the parking garage, her stay in the hospital, her and Brad's wedding and their life together. Then she recounted the awful months leading up to Mary's birth, their separation and his subsequent death. She told him of her regrets, what-if scenarios and what were her wishes up until a couple of months ago. "I'm finally at peace with our life. I know Brad would want me to be happy, Edward. And I'm finally with someone with whom I feel like I can find that happiness," Kate hesitated unsure if she wanted to tell him her last secret. Taking a steading breath, she decided to just go with it and put it all out on the table. "I've fallen head over toes in love with you, Edward. Some days it scares the shit out of me. But most of the time it fills me up with such joy, I feel like I'll burst from it," Kate admitted quietly.

Edward had stilled when she told him of her feelings. Love? They'd only known each other a short time. Was it possible? Chuckling quietly to himself, he nodded his head. He knew it was. His parents had fallen in love with each other after only an hour. He could sense that Kate's feelings were real, and she believed in them whole-heartedly. Did he feel the same? His head was full of her, and had been since the first night they'd met. He barely went five minutes without thinking of her, wondering what she was doing, how she was feeling, when he'd be able to spend more time with her. He hadn't looked at another woman since he'd met her, though plenty had thrown themselves at him. The thought of losing her made him feel physical pain. He was scared as well, but the joy that Kate had just spoken of quickly filled him as well. Oh yes, he was definitely in love. With Kate and her precious daughter, Mary.

"And I love you, Kate," Edward said earnestly.

Sighing with happiness, Kate raised her head seeking out Edward's lips. Only to happy to oblige her, Edward showed her exactly how much he loved her.

"MOMMY!!!"

Kate startled awake, momentarily lost and unsure of her surroundings.

"I'll get her," Edward said as he jumped off the couch. He quickly threw on his jeans and ran out of the library.

Kate fumbled as she pulled on her clothes and then she

followed Edward out of the library.

She found Edward and Mary sitting on the stairs about halfway up. Mary was clinging to Edward, her face wet with tears.

Kate rushed up the steps. "What's wrong," she asked.

"I don't know. She won't say anything," Edward said, worry making his voice gruff.

Kate sat down next to Edward and stroked Mary's hair. "Baby, what's wrong?"

"M-M-Monster," Mary stuttered. Fear was evident in her eyes when she glanced at Kate.

"She's shaking like a leaf, Kate." He shifted Mary over to Kate's waiting arms, and trailed his hand down Mary's hair. "I'm going to go check out her room. You two stay here," he said as he climbed up the stairs.

Kate watched him go as she whispered soothing words into Mary's ear. They sat together on the steps, Kate rocking Mary back and forth as they waited for Edward to return. It seemed like hours, but was actually only a few minutes, and Kate's breath rushed out in relief when Edward rounded the corner.

"All clear," Edward said.

Kate stood with Mary. Edward leaned down and picked Mary up. Holding her close, he explained what he didn't find in her room. "I didn't find one single monster in your room, Mary. The windows were closed and locked, the door to the hallway was closed. I looked under your bed and only found a couple of dust bunnies. Nothing in the closet except some old clothes and shoes. How about we all go up and give it another search before you go back to bed?"

Whimpering, Mary shook her head and clung to Edward's neck.

"No? Would you rather sleep somewhere else tonight?"

"With Mommy," Mary whispered as she nodded her head against Edward's chest.

At Kate's nod, Edward carried Mary the rest of the way up the stairs. When they entered Kate's room, he gently laid Mary down in the bed. Pulling the covers up over Mary, he bent down and kissed her cheek. "Sleep well, princess," he whispered.

Rising, he stared at Kate for a moment. Kissing her cheek, he whispered in her ear. "Wish I was as lucky as Mary tonight."

Kate giggled. "If I remember correctly, you were very lucky this evening already," Kate whispered back. "There's always tomorrow," she promised.

"Until then." He bent down and gave her a quick, but delicious, kiss on the lips. "Sleep well, my love."

"You too," Kate said as she watched him go.

Quickly changing into her pajamas, she snuggled in bed with her daughter.

"Would you like me to sing you to sleep?" Kate asked quietly.

"Yes please," Mary said as she burrowed closer to Kate.

As she sang, Kate's mind wandered back to the library and the time she had spent with Edward that evening. All their secrets were out and she couldn't be happier with it. Well, she wouldn't lie to herself and say she was totally thrilled with Edward's career. But she loved him, and they'd somehow make it work. She was glad they had a plan of action to deal with the paparazzi for Mary's sake.

She was having a hard time believing he was famous. He was so down to earth and nice, not at all what she envisioned a famous actor to be like.

The best part of the evening though, was when he admitted he loved her. She's been a little nervous, okay a lot nervous, when he'd hesitated after she'd told him her feelings. She'd been worried that he wouldn't return her feelings, but when she heard him say the words, with so much of his heart in the words, she knew he meant it. And then when he'd shown her how much he loved her, who could doubt?

She had no idea where they'd go from here. Her life was in the States, and his was here in London. Kate wasn't sure if she was prepared to leave everyone she knew and loved to make a new life here. Shaking her head, she scolded herself. She was getting too far ahead of the game. There was no marriage proposal or any talk of moving in together. She needed to get a handle on her imagination. Oh, but a girl could dream...and dream is exactly what Kate did.

Chapter Twenty-Four

"Mommy, why are you crying?" Mary asked as she hugged Kate's leg.

Kate quickly swiped at her tears and put her arms around Mary. "Oh," Kate let out a chuckle. "I didn't notice I was. I guess I'm just sad to be going home."

"Don't you want to go home, Mommy? What about Ah G? And Uncle Tim? And Gram? And Ms. Erin?" Mary asked worriedly.

"Oh darling, it's not that I want to stay, it's just that I'll miss Edward." Kate kissed the top of Mary's head. "Won't you?"

Mary nodded. "Will Edward come visit us again?"

"I'm sure he will. I think Edward will miss us just as much as we'll miss him!"

"You're mother speaks the truth, Mary," Edward said as he entered the room. "I've enjoyed having you both here so much."

Both Kate and Mary jumped when they heard Edward's voice. Kate turned and smiled at him as Mary ran over to give Edward a hug. Edward lifted her into his arms and held her close whispering his plans for a visit very soon.

Kate gave up on packing and walked over to them. She needed to feel Edward's arms around her too. She sighed as she felt Edward's lips on her head. It was going to be hard to leave him.

Six weeks was a long time to go without seeing the one you love. Never mind that his time had been filled, Edward missed Kate and Mary. His latest film project had been postponed since the lead actress had literally broken a leg on the set. James had succeeded in clearing Edward's schedule for the six months Edward had requested. So he'd taken his mother on a cruise of the Caribbean sooner than they had planned. Edward hadn't seen the point in waiting until the dead of winter when they both had the time and energy to go sooner. He had wanted to rent a yacht and hire a captain, but his Mum had insisted on a good old-fashioned cruise. They'd been at sea for fourteen days and initially he'd been worried about constant interruptions from fans asking for pictures and autographs. But he'd been pleasantly surprised when after the second day, he'd been largely left alone. He was further surprised when he had found himself enjoying the food, activities and the relaxation. So surprised, in fact, that he found himself wanting to take Kate and Mary on a cruise in the near future. He'd gotten into a lengthy discussion with the activities director about the pros and cons of a cruise with children, the best kid-friendly cruises and the best times to go with children. She had pointed him toward the Disney cruise line, indicating he'd never regret it.

The weather had been amazing. Sun everyday and an occasional short rainstorm in the afternoon. Edward had spent quite a bit of time sitting on the deck pretending to read. Mostly he'd been staring out at the sea trying to figure out what he wanted to do with the rest of his life. And how he could convince Kate that she belonged in his life.

It was on one of these days, his Mum had foregone her usual activity of playing cards with some of the other widows on board the ship. She sat beside him on the deck.

"Penny for your thoughts, dear?"

"Hi Mum," Edward smiled at her. "No cards today?"

"No, I thought I'd spend some time with my son today."

"Brilliant! What should we do?"

"I thought we could start by discussing whatever has you staring out at sea day after day."

Edward chuckled. "Well, I'm just trying to figure out what I want to be when I grow up. And how Kate and Mary fit in."

"Hm, I thought you were already grown up?" Charlotte said. "And I'd say Kate and Mary fit in rather perfectly. So, what really has you staring out to sea so solemnly?"

"I just don't know if my career is conducive to a strong relationship. And if it's not, am I willing to do something different so that my relationship with Kate doesn't suffer. She's a private person, which I respect, and I don't want to intrude on her life and steal Mary's childhood. I'm quite a lot to take on, Mum."

Charlotte laughed. "That you are, my boy, that you are." She patted his arm. "Have you asked Kate how she feels about your career and your baggage?"

He nodded. "As long as Mary is safe and kept out of the spotlight as much as possible, she's fine with it. She says it's who I am and she's not out to change me. My problem is that I'm not in control of the media and I'd die if something were to happen to Mary."

"What would you do instead of acting?"

"I don't know. I've thought about directing, or theater work or writing a book," Edward said shaking his head. "I've no idea, really. Acting is all I know. It's all I'm good at!"

"You could always retire," Charlotte said softly.

"Retire? Me? I'm a little young to be thinking that, don't you think?" Edward asked incredulously.

"Well, for normal people, yes. But you've more money than the queen and you've invested it well. You really have no reason to work except to escape the boredom of everyday life. Though with a family, I doubt you'd get bored."

"True. But what's my next step? Normally people try out living together for awhile. Kate and Mary live on the other side of the ocean. That's not really conducive to trying it out." He was frustrated by all the questions with no answers and his tone indicated that.

"That's a hard question, but one you should probably discuss with Kate. She'd be the one with the best answer to this, as she knows what they need." Charlotte sat up, looked him in the eyes as she reached for his hand. "Or, you could ask her to marry you."

"Marry me?" Edward shook his head. "Oh, I don't think we're ready for that. Kate wouldn't rush into something that permanent so quickly. She has Mary to think about."

"Quickly? You've known each other for six months. How is that quickly?"

"Mum! Not everyone is like you and Dad. Or Meaghan

and Rufus. Or even Aunt Imogen and Uncle Walter. Most people, rational, sane people, wait a year or two or five before getting married."

"They're stupid. You know what you know and an extra year or two or five isn't going to change anything," Charlotte said exasperated. "Do you love her?"

Edward rolled his eyes. "Yes."

"Does she love you?"

"Yes."

"Then the solution is simple." Charlotte narrowed her eyes and stared hard at him. "At least it should be."

Edward nodded and smiled at his mother. "Thanks, Mum."

Now he was on a plane, bound to see the two loves of his life, and still unsure of what he should do. His path wasn't clear in his mind and that scared him as he wasn't one to be indecisive and unsure of himself. What was clear was his determination to make Kate and Mary his priority. He'd find a niche for himself somewhere when the dust settled.

This morning before leaving for the airport, he'd gone to his favorite jeweler's and had his mother's engagement ring reset to make it unique for Kate. The original diamond was square cut, and he'd had the jeweler put in an oval sapphire on either side of the diamond. The ring itself was platinum, and Edward had the jeweler buff it up to a beautiful shine. He was happy with the end result and hoped Kate would like it.

He wasn't sure if Kate was ready for him to propose, but he wanted to be prepared in case the opportunity presented itself. He'd also gotten Mary a heart shaped locket and had put a picture of the three of them inside it. It was a picture that his Mum had taken while they'd been at his house. He wasn't just asking Kate to marry him, he was also promising to be a father to Mary and he wanted her to feel just as special and loved by him as Kate did.

A few hours later, Jason dropped Edward in front of Kate's apartment building and then continued on to the hotel where he'd stay unless Edward needed him. After saying goodbye to Jason, Edward picked up his luggage and headed into the lobby of Kate's building.

"Edward Kent?"

Edward turned his head and pinned the man with a glacial stare. "Yes?"

"Sir, I'm Brent from *The Moon...*"

"*The Moon*," Edward interrupted. "What are you doing here?"

"Sir?" The reporter asked.

"Why. Are. You. In. America?" Edward ground out slowly between clenched teeth. "You're a British rag, this is not Britain."

"Sir, with all due respect. You're a super star. One that's dropped off the radar. I'm here to find out why."

Edward stepped up into the reporter's face. "How long have you been here?"

"Er, two and a half weeks," the reporter said hesitantly. He took a small step backwards.

"Have you been camped in this lobby the whole time?" Edward asked menacingly.

"Sir, what is your relationship with Kate Walker?" Brent asked avoiding the question.

"I asked you a question, Brent," Edward said softly as he took another step closer to Brent.

Brent took a step backwards. "Yes, sir. I have been camped here in the lobby."

Nodding slowly, Edward stepped into the reporter's space again. "My relationship with Kate Walker is none of your business," he said in a dangerously soft whisper. "You want to talk about my latest movie, or my charitable organizations, ask away. But my personal life, as far as you're concerned, is closed."

Edward turned on his heel and walked to the bank of elevators, missing the calculated gleam that entered the reporter's eyes as Edward walked away.

Fuming, he pulled his cell phone out of his pocket as soon as the doors to the elevator closed.

"Edward..."

"Why is there a reporter from *The Moon* camped in Kate's lobby, James?" Edward interrupted. "He's been here for two and half weeks!"

"Yes sir, I know."

"I beg your pardon?"

"Sir, with all due respect. You were on vacation with your mother..."

"James, I didn't take you for an idiot."

"Sir?"

"When I told you that I didn't wish to be disturbed, that wasn't to mean you didn't inform me of important issues. A reporter, camped in Kate's lobby for two and a half weeks, is an important issue," Edward explained in a slow voice as if he was speaking to a child.

"Yes, sir. I apologize."

Edward sighed. "What's the story, James?"

James cleared his throat. "Ah, they're saying you had some sort of breakdown. I've been working with your publicist, Gretchen, to get to the bottom of it. All the rags are going crazy right now for info."

"Why would they think I've had a breakdown?"

"I think it has something to do with me rearranging your schedule for six months. The director of Pride and Prejudice was not happy with the delay."

"You did tell him that I would gladly give up my spot in the movie?"

"I did, and he took me up on it at first. But when he broke the news to Olivia Kimball, she quit. She wanted you to be her leading man and no one else would do. Rather than have to replace the both of you, he agreed to the delay," James explained.

"And I suppose someone in his camp called the rags and tattled?"

"That's what we suspect, Edward. We're still trying to pin down the tattler."

Edward thought about the best course of action. He wanted to put the rumors to rest, but he also didn't want to drag Kate and Mary any further through the mud. "Ok, here's what I want you to do. Forget about finding the tattler. Call *The Times* and give them an exclusive. Tell them I'll call tomorrow around two o'clock. I'll explain about my need for a break. Hopefully, that will take care of the problem and see the reporter from *The Moon* removed from Kate's lobby."

"Yes sir."

"And James. I want you to work on a press black-out for the rest of my vacation. Understood?"

"I'll get right on it, Edward."

Edward hung up and let out a deep breath. His next call was to Jason. After explaining about the reporter, Jason promised to take care of it. He prayed the idiot reporter downstairs hadn't ruined his fragile relationship with Kate. Two and half weeks? He couldn't believe someone hadn't called him about it.

Taking another cleansing breath, Edward knocked on Kate's door.

Chapter Twenty-Five

At the knock on the door, Kate glanced up warily. She'd sent Mary to Georgie's for the weekend, hoping that with Edward scheduled to arrive back in London from his cruise, the media would go away.

She'd been upset at the intrusion to her life, not expecting it here in America, where Edward wasn't as popular. But, if an A-List actor goes 'missing', she supposed it was going to make news everywhere.

The reporter had been camped down in the lobby for the better part of two weeks. He stopped Kate each time she went through the lobby, asking for information that she didn't have. It wasn't her place to give away Edward's secrets, not that she would anyway. Everyone was entitled to some privacy in their life, including those that choose to be a public figure. Her opinion was that the media didn't need to know everything that went on in a person's life.

The past few days, Kate had taken the elevator down to the parking garage and out the back way. She'd avoided the lobby altogether. The guy gave her the creeps and she didn't want him following her to the apartment.

She walked slowly over to the door, making as little noise as she could. Peering through the peephole, she gave a startled gasp when she realized who it was she was seeing. She threw open the door and flung herself into Edward's arms. "You're here!" She sighed into his neck.

"Hey!" Edward stumbled a little, dropped his bag and held her close. "You okay?"

"Yes, now that you're here. I've missed you!"

Suddenly remembering where she was and who was downstairs, she quickly stepped away from him. Glancing down the hallway, she pulled on his arm. "Let's get inside, quick."

Shutting the door behind Edward, Kate let out a sigh of relief.

"Has he been bothering you?" Edward asked her.

"He was, but a few days ago I started avoiding him. I sent Mary to Georgie's for the weekend. I was hoping the guy would go away since you were getting back."

"I've got Jason on it now." He ran his hands through his hair in frustration. "I'm so sorry, Kate."

Kate put her arms around him in comfort. "It's okay. We're okay," Kate soothed. "I wasn't expecting it to happen here," Kate said softly.

"Yeah, I know. Me either."

Shaking off the stress of the reporter's presence, Kate grinned at Edward. "What are you doing here?"

Returning the grin, Edward kissed her lips. "I missed you."

"I'm so glad you're here. Mary is going to freak!"

"Are you really?" Edward asked. "Glad I'm here, I mean?"

"Oh Edward, I am. Truly. The intrusion was tolerable and required me to change my comings and goings. It wasn't something I can't live with."

"But you had to send Mary away, that can't have been easy for you."

"Well, it wasn't and I didn't have to send her away. I chose to because I thought she'd have more fun over there this weekend, than being cooped up here in the apartment. Besides, she hasn't spent a lot of time with them since we got back. I've been working a lot and Georgie really wanted some quality time. I even thought about joining them tomorrow, for a change of pace. But, you're here now and that really does make my heart happy."

They snuggled on the couch for awhile, catching each other up on their lives over the past six weeks. When Edward's stomach growled, Kate glanced up at him. "Hungry?"

"Starved. I think I had breakfast, at least that's the last

meal I remember."

Kate jumped up. "Why didn't you say anything? Let's go get some dinner, then!"

Edward grabbed her hand and led her to the bedroom. "Let's get gussied up and go somewhere fancy," he suggested.

"Edward, I don't need fancy."

Placing his hands on either side of her face, he gently brushed a kiss across her lips. "I know." He kissed her again. "But I love you, and I want to take you out. Please?" He kissed her again.

Kate sighed against his mouth. "Alright, Edward."

Smiling, Edward reached for her hand and continued to the bedroom. They got dressed quickly and while Kate was putting the final touches on her makeup, Edward called down for a limo.

"Ready," Kate twirled as she walked into the living room. "How do I look?"

"Stunning," Edward smiled appreciatively. "Absolutely stunning."

Grinning, Kate picked up her purse. "So, where are we going?"

"It's a surprise," Edward said mysteriously. Winking at her, he opened the front door and motioned her forward. "You take my breath away," Edward whispered against her ear as she walked by him.

Shivers raced down Kate's spine. She stopped short and leaned into Edward. She raised her lips and sank into a kiss that made her heart race with excitement. "Are you sure you want to go out?" Kate asked with a smirk.

"Ah, you tempt me," Edward said against her lips. "But I have something special planned. Come on, let's go."

They snuck out the back of the building in case the reporter had made his way back to the lobby. Settling themselves into the limo, Kate snuggled up to Edward. He wrapped his arm around her and kissed her softly against her temple.

"So," Kate whispered. "What is this something special you have planned?" She felt Edward smile against her skin.

"It's a surprise, my love."

It was dark outside and the street lights were twinkling. The weather had turned brisk the past few days and Kate could imagine snow gently falling along the streets. She loved the snow and thought it would make this evening perfect.

She was definitely surprised when they pulled up in front of her favorite Italian restaurant, Emilio's. She hadn't been paying attention and while Emilio's was only a couple of blocks from her apartment, it seemed the driver had taken them on a long cut to get here. She smiled to herself, it was thoughtful of Edward to do that. She hadn't exactly been shy in her appreciation of the limo he'd gotten her and Mary in London.

The driver came around and opened their door. Edward exited the limo and reached in to help Kate out. She smoothed her dress and clasped Edward's hand.

The familiar aromas of Emilio's wrapped themselves around Kate as they walked inside. She breathed deeply and wasn't surprised when her mouth immediately watered.

"Kate! So happy to see you!" Nan said as she kissed Kate's cheek.

"Hello Nan! You remember Edward?"

"Of course, Edward!" Nan kissed his cheek as well and then gestured into the restaurant. "I have your table ready," she said as she picked up their menus. Nan led them to their table and then quickly withdrew.

Kate gasped quietly as she took in the scene. A dozen red roses sat in the center of the table. A bottle of champagne was chilling by the table. Two white candles were flickering next to the roses.

Heart melting, she gazed up at Edward and smiled hugely. "This is so lovely, Edward." She rose up on tiptoes and brushed a kiss against his mouth. "Thank you," she whispered.

"You are most welcome," Edward said as they both sat down.

Kate leaned forward and smelled the flowers. "So beautiful," Kate remarked.

Gazing intently at her, Edward smiled. "I was just thinking the same thing, but not about the flowers. You put them to shame."

Kate reached for his hand and linked her fingers with his. "I feel like I should pinch myself."

"No need, love. I promise you this is real."

Nan returned and poured their champagne. Kate picked up her glass. "To real life," she said.

"And forever," Edward finished.

Raising her glass to her lips, she closed her eyes as the champagne slid down her throat. It was cool, crisp and slightly fruity. Taking another sip, she slowly opened her eyes to find Edward kneeling next to her. He held a small black box with a beautiful diamond and sapphire ring nestled inside.

"Kate, you are my love and the only woman I want to spend the rest of my life with. I want to watch Mary grow up into a wonderful woman, I want to sleep beside you every night and I want to grow old with you. Will you make me the happiest man in the world and marry me?"

Kate felt tears sliding down her cheeks at the same time her face lit up in a smile. Nodding her head and reaching for Edward, she crushed him into a tight hug. "Yes, yes, yes! I love you, Edward." She said against his ear.

Still holding the ring, Edward wrapped his other arm around her to return the hug. "I love you, Kate." Edward pulled back a little and slid the ring on Kate's finger.

"Oh Edward, it's so beautiful! Thank you!"

The ringing of Kate's phone interrupted the moment. She glanced questioningly at Edward. "Go ahead. Answer it," he said.

Kate pulled it out of her purse. "It's Georgie," Kate said before flipping it open. "Hello?"

"Oh my God, Kate!" Georgie dissolved into hysterical sobs.

"Georgie! What's wrong? What's happened?"

Kate could hear Tim yelling Mary's name in the background. "Georgina!" Kate exclaimed as she jumped to her feet. Grasping the phone tight to her ear, she yelled into the phone. "What has happened? Where's Mary?"

Edward stood up and reached for Kate's phone.

"Georgie, it's Edward. What's going on?"

"She's gone."

"What do you mean? Where?"

"I don't know," Georgie sobbed. "She was right here, between Tim and I and now she's gone."

"Where are you?"

"At the convention center," she said before dissolving into hysterical sobs again.

"We'll be right there," Edward said. He grabbed Kate's hand and started toward the door.

She watched as he made a quick call on his cell and as he took care of the bill with Nan by passing her his credit card as they rushed through the restaurant. "Edward, what's going on?" She asked as they raced through the door.

He didn't answer her until they were out on the sidewalk. He swept his eyes up and down the street and then settled them on her. He took her hands in his and very gently told her what was going on. "Mary is missing."

It took a moment for the words to sink in. "What?" Kate asked as tears coursed down her cheeks. "What did you say?" Kate yelled as she pushed out of Edward's arms.

"Georgie said Mary was standing between her and Tim and now she's gone."

"My baby," Kate whispered. She bent over at the waist, gulping in huge amounts of air. "I can't breathe," she gasped.

The limo stopped at the curb and Edward scooped her up and set her down on the seat. He told the driver where to go and then pulled Kate into his arms. "We'll find her, Kate. I promise."

The drive to the convention center was the longest of Kate's life. She trembled the entire way, her mind racing with hundreds of unpleasant possibilities.

Kate was out the door before the limo came to a stop. She raced to the doors and was stopped by a security guard. "I'm sorry ma'am. You can't come through here. No one in or out."

"Let me through," Kate screamed at him. "It's my baby!" She tried to push past him, but the security guard held her back.

"I'm sorry, ma'am. I can't let you through."

Edward caught up to Kate and took her hand. "Look, Georgie is across the way," Edward pointed.

"Georgie!" Kate yelled when she saw her sister.

"Kate!" Georgie and Tim ran toward Kate, with what looked like cops following behind. After a quick exchange of words, Kate and Edward were finally admitted through the doors.

"What happened?" Kate asked brokenly, as she walked into Georgie's arms.

"We aren't sure," Tim said. "She was standing between us. We were watching the clowns do a football routine. Georgie reached down to take Mary's hand and ask her if she could see. She wasn't there. We'd only been standing there for a minute or two. I don't know if she wandered off and got lost, or if someone took her."

"Security guards were alerted right away?" Edward asked.

"Yes," Tim nodded. "Georgie was screaming for Mary and a guard came right over as we were looking around for her," Tim pointed to one of the two people who had followed them over. "He called the police and started the security procedures or whatever. The cops came minutes later."

"What do we do now?" Kate asked the group. "How do we find Mary?"

The other man stepped forward. "I'm Officer Finney," he said. Then he looked at Kate and Edward. "I need to speak with Ms. Walker."

The officer led Kate and Edward a few feet from Georgie and Tim. Edward held Kate's hand, giving her as much support as he could.

"I wasn't here. I don't know what I can tell you," Kate said. "I just want my baby girl back."

"Ms. Walker, I understand you were at dinner with Mr. Kent?"

"Yes. What does that have to do with anything?"

"Is it normal for your sister to care for your child?"

"Excuse me?" Kate said icily. "Are you suggesting Georgie did something to Mary?"

"I'm just asking questions, ma'am."

Kate took a deep breath and let it out in a rush. "Yes, it's normal. Georgie and Tim take Mary for an overnight or a whole weekend, once a month. I'm a single mother and they can't have children. It's a win-win situation, sort of. I get a break and they get to spend quality time with their niece."

"Have they taken Mary to the circus before?"

"Yes, they go every year. It's their special thing."

"Does anyone else know about this annual event?"

"Of course. I know, my parents know, some of our friends know. Edward knows."

"Would any of the people who know have a reason to take Mary?"

"What?" Kate exclaimed. "No! Why are you asking?"

"Ma'am, this was found on your sister's chair. Do you recognize the handwriting?"

Kate looked at the note and gasped. There was a blurred photo of Mary and Kate at the airport in London. Beside the photo, a note was written in neat, small block letters.

Five million dollars will ensure her safe return. Details to follow.

Kate handed the note back to Officer Finney and shook her head. "I don't recognize the handwriting."

Memories from the past months flooded Kate's mind. Flashes of light while she and Edward dined. People just on the edge of her vision, quickly disappearing when she would try to focus on them. The grainy picture of them kissing in the magazine Edward had shown her. The journalist camped in her lobby the past two weeks.

Slowly she turned to Edward. "It's because of you," she whispered, trembling. Red-hot rage was quickly replacing her fear and she welcomed it.

"Kate?" Edward asked in confusion.

She was no longer able to hold back her emotions. She raised her fists and beat them on his chest. "It's because of you that Mary is gone!" She screamed in his face. "This note proves it!" She flipped her hand toward the note that Officer Finney held. "That's us in London, Edward, when Mary and I were on our way back to the States." Kate continued her assault on Edward's chest. "No one would care about us if you weren't THE Edward Kent."

Edward grabbed a hold of her wrists. "Kate, please!" he implored.

"Don't touch me!" Kate screamed at him as she wrenched her wrists from his grasp. "It's your fault she's gone!" Kate turned on her heel and walked away from Edward. When she got to her sister's side, her knees buckled and she collapsed in a heap on the floor. Giant sobs wracked her body.

Edward followed her and dropped to his knees beside her. He wrapped her in his arms and placed a soft kiss on her temple. "We'll find her, Kate. I promise."

"What's going on, Edward?" Georgie demanded.

"A note was left on your chair. It was a picture of them at the London airport and demanding five million dollars for the safe return of Mary," Edward explained.

Georgie's face paled. "Five million dollars? Where will we get the money?"

Edward sighed. "From me, Georgie."

"You?" Georgie asked in confusion.

"Didn't Kate tell you? I'm Edward Kent, *The* Edward Kent. Europe's famous a-list actor and most eligible bachelor," Edward explained bitterly.

Georgie's mouth dropped open. "Seriously?"

Kate raised her head and glared at Edward. "Yes, seriously."

"Kate, you're blaming Mary's abduction on Edward's fame?" Georgie asked incredulously.

Kate moved out of Edward's grasp and stood on her feet. "Yes. We were nobody's. We'd still be nobody's." Kate glanced off into the distance. "I wish I'd never gone in that restaurant."

Georgie gasped. "Kate! You don't mean that!"

Kate's gaze snapped to Edward's. "Oh, but I do," Kate said

as she removed the ring Edward had given her less than an hour before. Holding it up, she placed it in Edward's shirt pocket. "Get my baby back and then get out of my life," Kate said.

And for the second time in less than ten minutes, Kate turned and walked away from Edward.

Chapter Twenty-Six

Edward stood rooted to the spot watching the love of his life walk away. She was right and he didn't blame her for her reactions. It was his fault Mary had been kidnapped and he'd do everything in his power to find Mary and bring her home to Kate.

But Kate was wrong if she thought he was going to let them walk out of his life. He loved them both to distraction and this situation only cemented his feelings. They were his life and he understood that to keep them safe and with him, he was going to have to make big changes in his life.

Officer Finney walked up to him, interrupting his musings. "Uh, sir. I need to ask you some questions."

"Fire away," Edward said.

"How long have you known the Walkers?"

"About nine months."

"How did you meet?"

"We met at a restaurant in London."

"You're from London?"

"Yes."

"And you're an actor?"

"Yes." Edward ran his hand through his hair in frustration. "Look, I know you have to ask these questions, but this isn't getting us any closer to finding Mary." Edward paced in a tight circle. "I need to call my bank and get started on the money transfer."

"Sir, there are procedures we must follow."

"Bloody Hell!" Edward growled, thrusting his hands through his hair. "Screw the procedures! I'm going to get Mary back."

"My captain will be here in a few minutes, sir. You can talk to him..."

A high-pitched scream interrupted Officer Finney. "Mary!" Kate screamed.

Edward ran over to Kate. "Kate, what's happened?"

"The kidnapper sent her a picture of Mary." Georgie said.

Edward grabbed Kate's phone.

"Is it another media picture?" Officer Finney asked.

"No," Edward said. His hand trembled as he showed Officer Finney the picture. "It's a current picture."

"Isn't that what she was wearing today?" Officer Finney asked as he flipped through his notes.

"Yes," Edward said. "This picture is from today." He scrolled down on the image. "And here are the instructions, Officer."

Officer Finney read the words aloud on the image.

Five million, corner of Isaac Street and Monroe Street.
6am tomorrow.
NO POLICE!!!
Mr. Kent and Ms. Walker - ONLY.

"Six am, tomorrow?" Kate said. "No! We need to find her NOW. I'm not going to stand around and let some monsters scare her. No!" Kate ran her hands through her hair. She stopped pacing in front of Edward and gazed up at him with pleading eyes. "Please Edward, I'm begging you. Find my baby. Please, bring her back to me!"

Edward reached out, wanting to feel their connection. But fearing another rejection, he dropped his hand at the last second. "I will, Kate."

"Officer Finney!" A large man strolled over to their group. He looked to be in his mid-fifties and had to be over six feet tall. He had a clean-shaven head, broad shoulders and dark chocolate eyes. He fixed his stare on Edward, even as he spoke to Officer Finney.

Officer Finney snapped to attention. "Sir!"

"Brief me," the man snapped.

"Sir. A six year old child was taken from the center stage. The victim and her guardians were taking in the pre-show festivities. The victim was standing between her aunt and uncle. When the aunt reached down to take the victim's hand, she realized the victim was missing. This note was left on their chairs, and a few minutes ago an image and instructions were sent to the victim's mother's phone."

The man inspected the note and the phone image. Handing both back to Officer Finney, he once again focused on Edward.

"You'd be Edward Kent?"

Edward nodded. "I am."

The man stuck out his hand. Edward took it, not surprised at the firm shake. "Captain Tom Driscoll." Dropping his hand, the Captain continued to eye Edward as he issued orders to Officer Finney.

"Officer Finney, we need to set up a command post. It can't be here, let's set up at the victim's home."

"Yes sir." Officer Finney ran off.

"Mr. Kent, I understand you'll be putting up the cash for the ransom drop?"

"Yes," Edward said.

"Well, let's get this started. I'll send a plainclothes officer with you," the captain said.

"Sir, with all due respect, that's unnecessary. I have my own security team and I'd prefer they accompany me to the bank."

The captain shook his head. "Everything I've heard and read about you made me think you were a logical and reasonable man," the captain said.

"Excuse me?" Edward sneered.

"Oh, you think I don't know who you are?" The captain grinned. "My wife is your number one fan, Mr. Kent. I've seen every movie and heard every piece of gossip concerning you. If it's to be found in the magazines, papers or on the Internet, my wife has heard about it and therefore so have I."

Edward grimaced. "I'm sorry to hear that, sir."

"Don't be. My wife needs something to occupy her time. Our kids are grown and I'm always at work." The captain crossed his arms and focused his intense stare on Edward's face. "Now, we need to get moving on this situation. I'll be taking Ms. Walker and her family back to her apartment. You go to the bank and get started on the money. Once you've finished at the bank, please join us at the apartment. We'll work on a plan for the drop."

Edward struggled with his emotions. There was no way he was letting the cops anywhere near this situation. The instructions had been clear and Edward wasn't going to allow them to mess up the drop. He and Kate would deliver the money, and if he could manage it, it would be his security people that would keep them safe.

"Sounds like a plan," Edward agreed.

The captain motioned to one of his officers. "Good luck, Mr. Kent."

Edward watched the captain walk over to Kate and Georgie.

"Sir, ready to go?" The officer asked.

"Yes," Edward nodded. He followed the officer into the lobby. "I need to use the restroom before we go," Edward said.

"We'll pass one on our way out. It's just down here a bit," the officer pointed further down the lobby.

Once they reached the restroom, Edward excused himself and went inside. He pulled out his phone and quickly dialed his bodyguard, Jason. He never traveled without him, but Edward rarely had to use Jason when he was visiting Kate. He couldn't believe he was having to use Jason, here in America, twice in a one day.

"Mr. Kent?"

"Mary's been taken. I'm on my way to Bank of America. Meet me there."

"On my way."

Edward hung up and walked back out to the waiting officer. "Let's go," Edward said.

Ten minutes later they pulled up in front of Bank of America. They both exited the car and walked into the bank.

"Hello sir, how may we help you today?" The lobby attendant asked.

"Hello. I need to speak with your bank manager."

"I'm sorry sir, he's gone home for the evening. We'll be closing in fifteen minutes."

"Get him on the phone, please. I need to speak with him."

"Sir, is this something that can wait until tomorrow morning?"

Edward pierced her with his cold stare. "If it could, I wouldn't be standing in front of you asking you to call him, would I?"

"Uh, no sir. I guess you wouldn't," she stammered. She

snatched up the phone and dialed. "Sir, this is Amanda Anderson. I have a gentleman here that would like to speak with you." She paused as the man on the other line replied. "Yes, I know sir, but he's very adamant."

Tired of waiting, Edward grabbed the phone from her. "This is Edward Kent, to whom am I speaking?"

"Richard Lenovo. I am the bank manager. What is the meaning of this?" The man asked indignantly.

"I suggest you get down here now as I am in need of a large amount of cash. My daughter has been kidnapped and I need to withdraw funds for the ransom."

"How much are we talking?"

"Five million. I need it by six tomorrow morning."

"Five million? There's no way we can accommodate you for that large a sum."

Edward held the phone to his chest and glared at Amanda. "Who's in charge of this bank?"

"Mr. Robbins. He's the bank president."

Edward hung up the phone. "Call him, now, please."

Edward watched as she dialed the phone again. "Hello, Mr. Robbins? This is Amanda Anderson at the bank. I have someone who needs to speak with you." She handed the phone to Edward.

"This is Edward Kent. I'm here at your bank and I'm in need of a large sum of money. My daughter was kidnapped and I need the money by six tomorrow morning."

"I'll be there in twenty minutes."

Edward passed the phone to Amanda. "He'll be here in twenty minutes," Edward said as he walked over and sat down in one of the lobby chairs.

The phone rang and Edward watched the color drain from Amanda's face when she answered. He could hear the bank manager's voice through the phone and it sounded as if Amanda was getting an earful. "Just hang up on him," Edward said loudly.

Amanda's eyes widened at his suggestion, but she continued to take the abuse. "Sir, there's no need. Mr. Robbins is on his way down here." Amanda winced as the bank manager piled more abuse on the defenseless lobby attendant. "Yes, sir." Amanda gently replaced the receiver and glanced at Edward. "He's on his way, too," she explained.

"Great, it'll be a party!" Edward said sarcastically.

"Not one that I want to attend," Amanda said. Color immediately infused her face as she realized what she'd said aloud.

Jason walked through the doors just then and Edward stood to greet him. "Thanks for getting here so fast," Edward said as he shook Jason's hand.

Jason nodded. Edward guided him over to the chairs. Sitting down, he quietly explained the situation and his wishes. Jason listened intently, only interrupting when he had a question.

"We need to get rid of this cop and somehow get Kate away from her apartment. All without the cops knowing or following. I don't want this drop screwed up, Jason. Mary's life depends on it."

Jason nodded. "Yes sir. When we're done here, let's go back to the hotel. We'll call in some of my men and get the plan worked out."

"Great. Let me go tell the cop to get lost and that I'll find my own way over to the apartment." Edward stood and walked over to the doors where the cop was waiting. "Officer, my bodyguard has arrived. Once I'm finished here at the bank, I'll be heading back to the hotel to get a change of clothes and then I'll head over to the apartment. I'm no longer in need of your services and I'm sure the captain has something that needs your attention."

"Sir, the captain told me to stay with you."

"Well, let's call your captain and see what he has to say," Edward suggested.

Edward watched the officer pull out his phone and dial. "Sir, Officer Wyatt here. Mr. Kent says his bodyguard will deliver him to the apartment when he's finished at the bank. Is there somewhere else I could be useful?" The officer listened intently to his captain. "Yes sir, I know you did, sir. No, I'm not questioning your orders, sir. That's why I'm calling, to get clarification. Yes sir. Thank you," the officer hung up and glared at Edward. "I'm not to let you out of my sight, Mr. Kent."

Edward smiled. "Splendid." He turned and walked back toward Jason. "No joy," Edward said to Jason.

"We'll figure out a way to get by him." Jason pulled out his phone. "Might as well make myself useful. I'll call in some favors and have them waiting for us at the hotel. How long do you think this will take?"

"I've no idea. The bank president should be here soon."

Jason nodded. "I'll have them waiting for us at the hotel." Jason walked away to make his calls and Edward watched him go with envy. He sorely wished he had something to do to take his mind off the situation and make him feel useful.

He sent a quick text message to Kate explaining where he was and what he was doing. He hoped her phone wasn't being monitored, but until he knew for sure, he'd have to keep his messages to the point. Done with that, he also sent a message to his mother. The last thing he wanted was her waking up to the news without hearing it from him.

A short man came through the doors. He hesitated a second as he scanned the lobby. His gazed settled on Edward and the man quickly walked over to him.

"Mr. Kent?" The man asked as he stuck out his hand toward Edward.

Standing, Edward clasped the man's hand. "Yes. You would be Mr. Robbins?"

Mr. Robbins nodded his head. "Come with me, it'll be easier to discuss this in my office."

"Sir?" Amanda interrupted. "Mr. Lenovo is on his way. Should I send him to your office?"

Mr. Robbins sighed and dropped his head. Shaking it once, he raised his head and looked at Amanda. "No, have him wait down here. I'll speak to him once we're done." he said and then turned and led the way to his office.

Mr. Robbins motioned for Edward to sit down when they entered his office. He glanced up at Jason and the officer apologetically. "I'm sorry I don't have more seats. It's not often I entertain more than one person at a time." He took his seat behind his desk, retrieving a piece of paper and a pen before glancing up at Edward. "Would you please fill me in on all the details?"

"Yes." Edward explained the ransom notes, Mary's abduction and the deadline and his willingness to pay the ransom. "I know you aren't my bank, but I figured you were the only bank around with the resources to help. I'm sure my bank would be willing to do a transfer."

"This won't be a problem. We definitely have the resources, and I'll work with your bank in London to replenish our funds. We have an account for such an occasion, not that we have to use it often. I think we've only used it twice since I've been president and both times the money was returned as the criminals were caught."

"I'm hoping we have the same outcome tomorrow, sir." Edward said.

"I need a number where I can reach you," Mr. Robbins

said. Edward gave Mr. Robbins his number, and Kate's as well. "I'll start the paperwork for this tonight and as soon as your bank in London opens, I'll be on the phone with them. Would you mind writing down the name of the person you usually deal with? It'll make things go smoother in the morning."

"Not a problem," Edward said as he wrote down the information. "I've also marked down my account number, in case you need it." Edward stood and shook Mr. Robbins hand. "I appreciate your assistance, Mr. Robbins."

"Anything you need, please don't hesitate to call. Here's my card."

"Thank you." Edward turned and walked out of the office, relieved to have this part of the situation under control.

Chapter Twenty-Seven

Kate couldn't get her mind to focus. She had gone straight to Mary's room when they had returned to her apartment. Tears streaked down her face as she stood in the doorway. Her eyes scanned the room and settled on Mary's lovey, a purple spotted cheetah they'd gotten at the zoo.

Kate walked over to Mary's bed and sat down pulling the cheetah into her arms. She remembered the day they'd gotten this cheetah. It had been shortly after they'd moved into the apartment. The weather had been beautiful, a warm day with almost no humidity. Not wanting to waste the day, Kate had decided to take them to the zoo.

They'd done the tour of the zoo, stopping for lunch at one of the cafés. They'd snacked on popcorn and cotton candy as well. And at the end of the day, they'd swung into the gift shop to pick up a small souvenir of their day. Mary had spotted the cheetah right away and pointed at it. When Kate picked it up, Mary had strained against the buckles in the stroller to hold it. Once Mary had gotten her hands on it, she hadn't let it go for days.

The cheetah wasn't left behind often, but with the reporter camped out and the spontaneous decision to send Mary to Georgie's, it was no wonder he'd been forgotten. Kate bent her head and inhaled Mary's unique child scent. Her tears fell in earnest as Kate sat clutching the cheetah to her heart. Slowly, Kate fell sideways on the bed, pulling her knees up and settling in the fetal position.

Closing her eyes she let her mind drift in and out of six years of memories. The moment she found out she was pregnant. The joy she and Brad had shared at the news. The initial shopping trip and the onesie Brad had held up with "Daddy's Little Girl" written on it. The day Mary was born and the moment Georgie had appeared in the hospital room declaring Mary the most beautiful child ever born. Mary's first birthday and how she'd been covered head to toes in frosting from her smash cake. The joy of life that Mary had and the unconditional love they shared. The way her eyes lit up on Christmas morning and her insistence that they put out carrots for the reindeer along with Santa's cookies and egg nog.

The way she'd trusted Edward on sight and had so easily fallen in love with him. The way she had listened intently to Edward as he showed her how to ride a pony that day at his home in England. And the way she would curl up at your side when listening to bedtime stories. The way her nose would scrunch when she didn't like something. And the way her eyes would dance when someone told her they loved her.

"Kathryn!"

Kate started at the stern voice coming from the door. She opened her eyes and focused on her mother as she walked into the room. She sat on the bed next to Kate and rested her hand on Kate's head, brushing the hair from her forehead.

"Kate, you can't hide in here," Barbara said soothingly.

"Mom, she's gone and I don't know what to do," Kate voice cracked.

"The police need your help," Barbara said softly.

"I know. But I can't help them. If I do, it'll make this real and I can't handle real, Mom. It's too much. I've been through too much and this is it. This is what breaks me."

"You know God doesn't give us more than we can handle."

"Mom, I can't. I just can't," Kate shook her head. "You and Georgie can answer any questions they have."

Barbara continued to sit and rub Kate's back. Kate's tears wouldn't stop. Barbara handed Kate a tissue and Kate clutched it in her hand along with the cheetah.

"Edward proposed," Barbara asked.

Kate groaned and nodded.

"You accepted and then changed your mind?"

Kate nodded again.

Her mother made a tsking noise. "Seems to me that man is doing more to find your daughter than you are right now. Doesn't seem like you're giving him a fair shake."

"He's the reason, Mom."

"Really?" Barbara shook her head. "What's your reasoning? He wasn't even there. You should be blaming Georgie and Tim, your logic is so convoluted."

"Mom!" Kate exclaimed. "It wasn't their fault!"

"How can you say that? They were there. They should have been watching her more closely. How can you blame a man who was asking you to marry him and not blame the people who were with her and supposedly watching her?"

"Because! If it weren't for him, no one would want her. No one would even know she existed!"

"Kathryn Faith Walker! That is the most ridiculous thing I've ever heard," Barbara said as she jumped to her feet. She pointed her finger in Kate's face. "You need to think long and hard about what you're doing. That man loves you and your daughter and something like that doesn't come around everyday. He's out there, fighting and working to find Mary and all you seem to be able to do is lay in here, clutching a toy and blaming him." Barbara walked to the door. "You're stronger and fairer than this, Kathryn. Pull yourself together, get out here and help us get Mary back!" She walked out and gently pulled the door closed leaving Kate to her thoughts.

Kate watched her mother leave the room. Rolling onto her back, Kate glared at the ceiling. Leave it to her mother to take away the one thing Kate had to be angry about. She still felt as if Edward were to blame, though to be fair, it was indirectly. It wasn't as if he called the kidnappers himself and set it up. And her mother was right, he was out there trying to get Mary back.

But Kate couldn't see past her fear for Mary. What if they never got her back? Or what if they did but someone else tried this again? When Kate thought it was just pictures being taken and reporters camping in lobbies, she could deal with that. Mary being kidnapped was a whole other beast and Kate wasn't willing to make that kind of adjustment to their life.

Kate had never been interested in the rich and famous. Even as a kid she'd been more interested in books and her friends. She never knew who the popular actors or musicians were. Never knew which movies were playing or which song was number one. When she wasn't playing with friends, she was reading or creating patterns for her pretend clothing line.

Georgie had been the one interested in all that. She could remember Georgie going crazy for all types of teenaged heartthrobs. The posters all over her walls and piles of keepsakes.

Even now, Georgie subscribed to all the gossip magazines and watched all the entertainment shows. She was very well-versed in who's who around the globe.

And just like that, everything clicked into place.

Georgie.

Georgie would have had to know Edward. As addicted to that realm as she was, there was no way Georgie hadn't known or heard about Edward. No way he had avoided her radar.

The circus had been a perfect opportunity. Plenty of people, plenty of exits. Georgie was well-acquainted with the layout of the convention center since they'd been to the circus a few times before.

But the biggest question was who took Mary? Witnesses placed both Georgie and Tim in the center-stage the whole time.

It really hadn't been Edward's fault, he'd been a pawn in this sick game. Kate felt a sudden urge to vomit. She'd given his ring back. She'd been so cold and furious with him. She'd told him she never wanted to see him again. How would she ever fix what she'd broken?

She shook her head. First she had to get Mary back, then she'd work the rest of her life to earn Edward back.

She placed the cheetah back on Mary's bed, in it's place of honor on Mary's pillow. She stormed out of Mary's room, eyes darting everywhere as she searched for her sister. Walking into the kitchen, she stopped just inside the door. Kate pinned Georgie with a furious stare.

The cops stood up, ready to ask Kate questions and Barbara walked over to place a hand on Kate's shoulder.

"Oh good, Kate. I'm glad you came to your senses," Barbara said.

Kate didn't spare her mother a glance. "Where's Mary?" Kate asked Georgie coldly.

"Kathryn!" Barbara scolded.

Kate held a finger up in her mother's face. Continuing to glare at her sister, Kate asked again. "Where's Mary?"

The cops separated. One to Kate's side and the other to Georgie's side.

"Kate!" Georgie exclaimed. "I have no idea."

Shaking her head, Kate advanced on her sister. Stopping directly in front of Georgie, Kate placed her hands flat on the table. In a low voice, Kate threatened Georgie. "You have five seconds to tell me where she is, or I will come across this table and..."

Barbara flew across the room and grabbed Kate's arm. "Kate! This is insane, what are you doing?"

Kate shrugged off her mother. Still glaring at Georgie, Kate answered her mother. "Georgie knows where she is mother. Don't let her fool you. She almost got away with it but while I was in Mary's room 'blaming Edward', I put it all together."

"Georgie would never do what you're suggesting, Kate," Barbara said. "She's always been there for you. You'll ruin your relationship if you continue with this."

"It's already ruined, isn't it Georgie?"

"You were going to take her away," Georgie said quietly.

Barbara gasped and sunk into one of the kitchen chairs. "Oh Georgina," she whispered.

"Where's Mary?" Kate asked calmly.

Georgie stared out the kitchen window. Sighing, she began her tale. "Of course I knew who he was from the first second I saw him. I couldn't believe you'd snagged the biggest star in England. And even more unbelievable you didn't even know who he was! But even then I could see how much he adored you and Mary. And I knew eventually you'd make it permanent. You love London and have since your first trip over there. And now you've met someone from London, it wasn't a far stretch to think you'd move there when you married."

"But Georgie, he just asked her tonight. There's no way you could have known in time to set this up!" Barbara said.

Still staring out the kitchen window, Georgie continued. "True, and I didn't know he'd propose tonight. This whole thing worked out better than I could have planned. Well, except for little miss know-it-all figuring it out. But he proposed, she gave the ring back and now it's well and truly over. They aren't going anywhere," Georgie laughed.

Barbara gasped at Georgie's cavalier attitude. "Georgina, what's happened to you?"

Georgie ignored her and continued. "That reporter has been camped downstairs and it wasn't any trouble to talk him into my plan. He needed a story and I was going to hand him one on a silver platter, if he helped me. When Edward arrived this afternoon and told him off, well Brent was even more happy to help me than before. He called me and we cemented the plan."

"The reporter!" Kate exclaimed. "I knew you had to be working with someone."

"Of course," Georgie said. "I needed an alibi and what was better than to be seen screaming for my 'missing' niece? Brent watched from the top of the stairs. When Tim and Mary headed down to center stage, I waved to him to let him know it was time."

"Why Georgie?" Barbara asked.

Georgie turned and faced Barbara. Pointing at Kate, Georgie snarled her answer. "She would have taken Mary and we'd never see her again. I barely get to see her now. Can you imagine if they'd moved to London?" she asked bitterly.

"Mary isn't yours, Georgie," Barbara said sadly.

"Where is she, Georgina?" Kate asked as calmly as she could. She was seething inside and wanted nothing more than to smash Georgie's smug face into the table.

Glaring at her sister, Georgie sighed. "The reporter has her in his van. He's waiting for me to call him and tell him where to take her for the night."

Kate barely spared her sister a glance. "Get her away from me," Kate said to the nearest cop as she pulled out her phone and dialed Edward.

He answered on the second ring. "Kate?"

"Georgie and the reporter took Mary. He's got her in his van," Kate said. "I'm so sorry, Edward."

"Jason and I will bring her home," Edward said.

"Thank you, Edward," Kate choked out, emotions making it difficult for her to speak.

"I love you, Kate. That hasn't changed. I'll call you when we're on our way home."

"Be safe." Kate hung up and paced her living room floor, stopping occasionally to glance out the window.

"Georgie, I'll call your father. He has connections, he'll find you a good attorney." Barbara said as the cops took Georgie out of the kitchen in cuffs.

"Katie..." Georgie pleaded.

Kate turned and stared at the shell that was her sister.

"I'm sorry," Georgie said.

Nodding, Kate sighed. "I know you are, but it doesn't change anything. You can't substitute Mary for your own child and I'm not going to sacrifice our happiness because you can't have children. I forgive you, but I won't forget and I don't want to ever see you again."

Turning her back on her sister and the mother who was so entirely on Georgie's side as usual, Kate put them out of her mind and started praying.

She prayed for Mary's safe return, for Edward and Jason to find Mary, for their safety and for Edward's forgiveness.

Kate shuddered to think what life would be like if Edward couldn't forgive her. She'd blamed him and pushed him away at the first sign of trouble. It wasn't a good indication of her ever-lasting love.

Kate heard the door close behind her signaling the departure of the cops, her sister and mother. Good riddance, she thought to herself. Not expecting anyone else in the apartment, she was startled to feel a hand on her shoulder. Turning, she was shocked to see her mother standing behind her. "Mom?"

Barbara pulled Kate into her arms. "Edward will find her, Kate."

Not accustomed to this kind of attention or affection from her mother, Kate just nodded against Barbara's shoulder.

"You thought I left," Barbara stated.

"Yes," Kate whispered.

"I'm sorry, Katie."

Kate looked questioningly at her mother.

"I'm sorry for allowing you to think she means more to me than you do. I love you both, equally, but I guess I've allowed you to keep me at arms length. You never seemed to need me as much as Georgie did. You were always so independent and sure of your path. She'll need help and we'll give it to her. But I can't do anything for her right now. You need me more than she does," Barbara explained.

Fighting back tears at this rare show of affection from her mother, Kate hugged Barbara tightly. "Thank you, Mom."

Barbara led Kate over to the couch as Captain Driscoll strolled out of the kitchen. He snapped his phone shut and directed a glare in Kate's direction.

"Kate, where's Edward?" he asked sternly.

"He's finding Mary, why?"

"He gave Wyatt the slip." He sighed and crossed his arms. "How did you figure out it was your sister?"

"It wasn't any one thing," Kate explained. "Thoughts and memories and things were just rolling through my mind. Her love of all things Hollywood, her obsession with television programs and magazines. It made me finally question how she could not have known him. He so famous, Europe's most eligible bachelor. She had to know. And then some of the things she said to me lately. How she'll miss us and how she had hoped to watch Mary grow up," Kate sighed. "I don't know, I just knew it was her."

He nodded as he wrote notes down in his notebook. "I have cars out looking for the van."

Kate shook her head. "Edward will find her."

He thrust his hand through his hair in frustration. "I just hope he doesn't get them killed."

Kate glared at Captain Driscoll. Unable to sit any longer, she walked over to the window. Offering more prayers for their safety and return, Kate closed her eyes and rested her forehead against the cool glass of the window.

Chapter Twenty-Eight

"I can't believe that worked," Edward said.

"Everyone has to use the loo at some point," Jason chuckled.

Laughing, Edward nodded and watched Jason check his phone when it chimed.

"Jolly says the van is in the mall parking lot. It's a few blocks from the convention center."

"Make him wait for us. Mary is scared enough. I want her to see a familiar face."

Jason nodded and quickly texted Jolly back with the instructions. At the next intersection, Jason made a u-turn and put the pedal down. They flew down the streets racing toward the mall.

"Shit, a cop," Jason said as he glanced in the rearview mirror.

"Good, let him follow. He can take care of the reporter for us."

"He'll get in the way," Jason grumped.

"Lose him then, but do it fast. We need to get to Mary."

"I'll just outrun him," he said as he pushed the gas pedal down even further.

"Bloody hell!" Edward swore as he was pushed back into

his seat. "I'd rather not die today, Jason."

Jason laughed, but continued to floor the car.

They arrived at the mall ten minutes later. Jason circled the mall and came in at the van from behind.

"What's the plan here?" Edward asked.

"Jolly is going to go for the guy and we're going for Mary."

Jason and Edward exited the car and met Jolly around the back of the van.

"We need to be quick. Cops followed us," Jason said.

Jolly quickly checked the clip in his glock. Satisfied with what he saw, he snapped it closed and nodded. "Ready."

Edward watched Jolly crouch and walk to the drivers side, staying out of the side mirror. His gun at the ready, he popped up, opened the door and pointed his gun at Brent. "Hands where I can see them!" Jolly said. He nodded at Jason when Brent's hands were secure.

Jason and Edward opened the back doors. Jason held back to allow Mary full sight of Edward.

Edward would never forget the sight in front of him as long as he lived. Mary was crouched up against the side of the van, panic etched on her face. Her hands were tied with rope and ducktape covered her mouth.

Rage for the treatment she'd received at the hands of Brent and Georgie coursed through him like wildfire. He wanted to rip the reporter to shreds with his bare hands. Some of what he felt must have shown on his face because he heard a small whimper come from Mary. Edward quickly smoothed out his features and knelt inside the van.

"Cops," Jason said nodding across the parking lot.

"Deal with them," Edward said. He slowly reached out toward Mary. "Shh, princess. It's going to be okay. I'm here to take you home. Let me free your hands." Edward quickly untied her hands and moved to the ducktape on her face. "I'm going to take the tape off now, it's going to hurt some. I'm so sorry, Mary."

Mary whimpered and tears coursed down her cheeks while Edward removed the tape. "I'm sorry, Mary," Edward repeated. When the tape was finally removed, he gathered her into his arms and held her close. "It's okay, Mary. You're safe now."

He continued to hold her close as he stepped out of the van. Nodding to Jason, he walked over and slipped into the backseat of Jason's rental car.

Whispering words of encouragement, he rocked her back

and forth, rubbing her back in small circles. Unwilling to let her go for even a second, he did his best to calm her and give her comfort.

Jason poked his head in the car. "They won't let me go until the Captain gets here."

Edward growled. "How long?"

"Says the Captain is on his way."

"Fine."

Edward watched as the cops cuffed Brent and put him in the back of the cruiser. He had a moment of regret that he wouldn't get his chance to pound the man into a pulp. But when Mary's head slipped off his shoulder, he glanced down at her sleeping face and knew his place was right here. Adjusting her position for more comfort for the both of them, he dropped a kiss on her temple and thanked God for keeping Mary safe.

Laying his head back against the seat, he hoped the Captain showed up soon.

"Kate? What's going on? Where is everyone? Where's the Captain going? Where's Georgie?" Tim asked as he entered the apartment.

"Oh, Tim," Barbara sniffled. "Sit down," she gestured toward the couch.

Kate turned from the window but didn't join them on the couch. "She's been arrested, Tim. I'm so sorry."

"Arrested? Why?" He asked as he looked from Kate to Barbara.

"She was behind Mary's kidnapping," Kate said sadly.

Tim jumped to his feet. "Are you crazy? She would never do something like that, Kate. She loves you and Mary so much."

Kate raised her hands and nodded. "I know she does. She was afraid that when Edward and I married, we'd take Mary to London and she'd never see Mary again."

"Oh my God," Tim groaned. He wiped his hand across his face and sat down heavily on the couch. "I can't believe she'd do something like this. I know she's had a hard time accepting that we aren't going to have kids, but I never in a million years thought she'd do something like this."

"I know, Tim. I can't think about her role in this. I'm keeping it together by a very thin thread," Kate told him.

"William is at the police station with her, Tim. He's

working on finding her a good attorney."

Tim turned a glacial stare on Kate. "You're going to let them prosecute her?"

"It's out of my hands, Tim. You know that. The cops are involved. It's kidnapping, I have no say now." Kate implored.

"Any good attorney will try to go with an insanity plea or whatever they're called now," Barbara told him.

Tim stood and headed for the door. "I'm heading over there to see what I can do for her," Tim said. Turning back to Kate, she could sense his anger radiating from him. "We did a lot for you, Kate. We took you both in and helped you get back on your feet. Don't let her suffer for this. She's ill, and needs help. Not jail." Tim turned and walked out, slamming the door behind him.

Kate let out a deep breath and turned back to the window.

"He's right, you know," Barbara murmured.

"Right, how?"

"She's ill. Not being able to have a baby has been so tough on her."

"That's no excuse to kidnap her niece, Mom. Can you imagine how scared Mary must feel? The terror she's been put through and how alone she is?" Kate shuddered and turned to look at her mother. "I had sympathy for her. Before she stole my child. There were other options. Adoption or foster care. They didn't have to choose being childless." Disgusted, Kate shook her head and turned back to the window.

"You'll turn your back on her forever?" Barbara asked gently.

"Probably not. She's my sister. But I'm furious and scared and I can't think beyond getting Mary and Edward back. I can't tell you what will happen," Kate said.

"Kate, please," Barbara pleaded.

"Don't push me, Mom. This wasn't something small like stealing my dessert. She kidnapped my child – that's a federal offense. It's like I told Tim, it's out of my hands. And be glad for it, Mom. Because with the way I'm feeling right now, I'd shoot her if I saw her."

Kate was glad when Barbara finally stopped talking. She was frantically looking up and down the street for any sign of Edward and Mary. He said he'd call when they were on their way, but it had already been so long. Trying to keep herself calm, she said another prayer asking for peace and their safe return.

"Captain is here," Jason murmured fifteen minutes later.

Edward lifted his head and sighed in relief. He watched the Captain stalk over to the car, and knew this wasn't going to be a pleasant conversation based on the look on the Captain's face.

"Mr. Kent, I thought we had an understanding?" The Captain said brusquely.

"We did, sir. But circumstances changed."

"Not in my book. Where is my officer?"

"I would assume still at the hotel, sir."

"And how did you get away him?"

"He had to use the loo," Jason offered, barely able to contain his grin.

The Captain glared at Jason. "I wasn't speaking to you."

Jason raised his hands in surrender and walked over to stand with Jolly.

"Look Captain," Edward said calmly, his patience almost at it's end. "We found Mary. She's safe and you have the bad guys in custody. You know if it had been your daughter, you would have done the same thing."

Rolling his eyes, the Captain braced his hands on the top of the car. "You could have gotten yourselves hurt. You could have gotten her killed," he growled.

Edward sighed. "But we didn't. And all I want to do right now is take Mary home and reunite her with Kate."

Sighing himself, the Captain nodded. "Welker!" he called to one of his officers.

"Sir?"

"Follow them back to Ms. Walker's apartment. Stay with them until I return."

"Yes, sir." Welker hurried off to his patrol car and pulled it around behind Jason's car.

The Captain walked over to Jason and Jolly and explained the situation to them. A minute later the two of them got in the car and within seconds they were on the way.

"Are we following the rules, here, Edward?" Jason asked.
"Yes."

Jason nodded and drove them to Kate's apartment.

Kate raised her head and blinked her eyes. She gave a strangled cry and clenched her hands into fists.

"Kate?" Barbara asked, hurrying over to Kate's side.

Holding her breath, Kate kept her eyes on the activity down below. She could see reporters and people milling about, crowding around a car and a cruiser that had just arrived.

She gasped when Edward emerged from the car holding Mary tightly to his chest. "He did it, he brought her home," Kate whispered.

"Oh Katie, look! It's Edward and Mary," Barbara exclaimed.

Barbara wrapped her arms around Kate and hugged her tight. Unable to stop the tears, Kate pressed her face into her mother's shoulder.

Jason opened the door and Edward walked through. He stopped just inside the entryway, eyes searching for Kate. She ran over to him and gazed into his eyes. The tears hadn't stopped and all she could see of him was a blurry outline. "Thank you, Edward," Kate choked out as she reached for Mary.

Edward gently relinquished his hold on Mary, placing her into Kate's waiting arms. "She's safe and unhurt, Kate. She fell asleep on the way here."

Kate's eyes drank in the sight of her sleeping child. Sitting down on the couch with Mary, Kate held her close and kissed her head. She ran her hands along Mary's body, checking for any signs she'd been hurt. Other than some marks on her wrists that looked like rope burn and some redness along her mouth, Kate could see that Mary was fine.

Kate's gaze found Edward, who was being enveloped in a bear hug from her mother. Her eyes roamed over his face ensuring he was also unhurt.

"Excuse me for one minute," Edward said gently working his way out of her mother's embrace.

Kate watched him walk to the kitchen and disappear through the doorway. She had so much to say to him, so much to apologize for, so much to thank him for. But she was glued to the couch, her fears unwilling to allow her to move. The weight of her child's body in her arms was something she never thought she'd feel again. The roller-coaster of emotions she'd been on for the past few hours made her feel exhausted and wrung out. She knew she wouldn't let Mary out of her sight for days and would most likely make Mary sleep with her for the next little while.

Barbara came over and sat beside Kate on the couch. She rested her hand on Mary's head, brushing her hair back from her face. "I'm so happy she's home safe," Barbara whispered.

Kate nodded. Her throat felt clogged with all the emotions and she knew no words would be escaping anytime soon. All she could do was sit on the couch and hold her precious child.

Barbara draped her arm around Kate and hugged her close. "Now that Mary is home, I'm going to go to the station and help out there," Barbara said. She placed a kiss on Kate's temple and slowly rose to her feet. "You and Edward need some time and I don't want to be in the way. Call me if you need anything and I'll come right back."

Kate nodded and offered a small smile for thanks. She watched her mother gather up her things. Barbara walked into the kitchen to say goodbye to Edward and hugged Jason on her way out.

When the door clicked softly behind her mother, Kate let out a sigh of relief. Her mother's uncharacteristic display of affection and unity had thrown Kate for a loop. She wasn't used to this behavior from her mother and wasn't really sure what to do with it. Her decision to go to the station now that Mary was home was more along the lines of what Kate was used to.

Edward emerged from the kitchen moments later. He walked over to Jason and spoke to him in quiet tones. Jason nodded and retreated to the kitchen. Edward walked slowly over to the couch and sat down.

"My plane leaves in an hour," Edward whispered. "I have a few things to do before I leave, but I just wanted to make sure you're going to be alright."

"Please don't go, Edward," Kate begged, her heart in her throat and fear shining in her eyes.

"Don't look at me like that, Kate." Edward implored. "I don't know what else to do. I am who I am. And if something like this were to happen again, I couldn't bear it."

Eyes brimming with tears that never seemed to end, Kate rested a hand on Edward's arm. "I'm so sorry, Edward. I'm so sorry I took my fear and anger out on you," she said quietly. "I overreacted and had no business blaming you for Mary's kidnapping."

"But you did," Edward said. "And I'm not sure I can live with the threat of losing you over something that might happen again."

Sobbing at the truth in his words, Kate shook her head. "No, Edward. I was so wrong. At the first sign of trouble, I flew off the handle and ran. And that's not who I am. I don't want us to be over. I want to grow old with you and love you for the rest of my life..."

"Kate, don't toy with me," Edward choked out.

"I swear to you, I'm not," Kate said earnestly through her tears. "I had a lot of time to think while Mary was missing. And I realized that I've been so happy since I met you. Yes, this whole thing scares me, but I'd rather be scared than alone. I need you, Edward."

"Forever, Kate?"

Unable to say a word with the emotions clogging her throat, Kate nodded.

Edward put his arm around her and pulled her close. "I don't want to be away from you, either of you, for one minute ever again," he said as he placed a hand on Mary's head and a kiss to Kate's temple. "I love you and Mary and you're stuck with me, forever."

"Oh, Edward. I love you too. Please, please forgive me," Kate pleaded.

"I do, though there's nothing to forgive." He reached into his shirt pocket and retrieved her engagement ring. "I believe this is yours," he smiled. Gently lifting her hand from beneath Mary's legs, he slid the ring back on her finger.

"Edward," Kate breathed. "Thank you. Thank you for forgiving me, for loving me, for loving Mary and for bringing her back to me. I'm yours, forever." Kate said fervently.

"Forever," he promised as he brushed his lips over hers.

Epilogue

A month later...

"Is this the last box?" Edward asked as he hefted it up into his arms.

"I think so," Kate said as she cast one last look around her apartment. She walked over to the window in the living room and gazed out for the last time. She would miss this little apartment. It had been her home for six years and so many memories had been made here. Sighing, she walked over to stand beside Edward.

"I'll take this down and give you a minute," Edward offered.

"No, it's okay. I'm ready," she said as she followed Edward into the hallway. "I'm ready to start our new life, with you."

Brushing a kiss across her forehead, Edward smiled. "Two more days."

"I know. I'm so excited. Do you think your mother has everything under control?" Kate asked worriedly.

"Are you kidding? She's in heaven."

Kate nodded. "Yeah, you're right." Stepping out onto the sidewalk, she felt tears sting the backs of her eyes. Her mother was hugging Mary tight and her father was overseeing the packing of the car.

"You'll call when you get there, no matter how late?" Barbara asked.

"Of course, Mom. But I'll see you tomorrow," Kate said.

"Are you sure you both don't want to fly over with us today?" Edward asked.

"We're sure. Georgie is being transferred to the mental health hospital this afternoon. We want to be there," William explained.

"I understand," Kate said. "Give her my love."

Tears brimming in Barbara's eyes, she hugged Kate close. "I will."

"Time to go," Edward announced.

A flurry of hugs and 'I love you's' and 'see you tomorrows' went around until they were finally seated in the limo. Kate waved to her parents as they pulled away from the curb.

"Are you okay, Kate?" Edward asked.

Nodding, Kate took his hand. "I am. I still can't bring myself to see her, but Georgie is getting the help she needs. I'm glad Tim is coming over with Mom and Dad tomorrow."

Edward squeezed her hand. "We can come back anytime you like, Kate."

"I know and I'm grateful."

"Mom, do I have to call Edward, Edward?"

"Well, what else would you call him?" Kate asked.

"Dad," Mary said rolling her eyes.

Kate and Edward gasped and exchanged looks. Edward cleared his throat. "Are you sure, Mary?"

Mary nodded. "You're marrying my Mom in two days. You're going to be my Dad now. It just makes sense."

Reaching over, he pulled Mary into his arms. "I would be honored if you called me Dad," Edward said gruffly.

Kate wiped the tears from her eyes. Life was as close to perfect as she could imagine. She was marrying a good man who loved her and Mary. They were moving to London. Edward had decided to quit acting and start directing. His plan was to take on one or two directing projects a year. He wanted to spend the majority of his days taking care of Mary, and if Kate wasn't mistaken, a new baby in eight months. Kate was positively giddy at the thought!

Erin hadn't wanted to lose Kate, so she created a position for her in the London office. Kate would still be in charge of marketing for the clothing lines, but she'd be focusing on the

European market. Kate was thrilled with this new challenge.

Yes, life was as close to perfect as it could get.

She reached for Edward's hand and smiled up at him. "To Fate," she murmured.

"To Forever," Edward replied as he leaned over and sealed his promise with a kiss.

Thank you for reading my debut novel!
I sincerely hope you liked it.
Please consider leaving a review on:
Amazon or Barnes & Noble.

My second novel, *Back to December,* is scheduled to be
released Spring/Summer 2014.

For more information about me, check out my website:
http://heathermccoubrey.com.
You can find me on Facebook at:
http://www.facebook.com/AuthorHeatherMcCoubrey.
And on Twitter & Instagram at:
@runmookiewrites.